"You still think I should go into hiding. Because I'm a woman."

Boyd rolled his shoulders. "You're a good cop."

"As if you're any judge," Melinda snapped.

"You're right. I want you out of this. You're dangling yourself out there like bait. Dorrance has already pinned his target on you. Because he blames you the most for his downfall? Because he resents that it was a woman who brought him down? Who knows. It doesn't even matter, because he doesn't just want to kill you. He wants you under his control! Do you know what that would do to everyone in this department? To me?"

And, God, he shouldn't have said that, because the shock on her face morphed into astonishment.

"You?" she whispered. "There's no reason—"

"There is, and you know it." He made himself look away from her and do some deep breathing. He hadn't meant to say any of this, was angry at himself for letting it get personal.

But it was. Damn it, it was.

Mustang Creek Manhunt deals with topics some readers might find difficult, such as sexual assault and the PTSD that follows as a result.

MUSTANG CREEK MANHUNT

USA TODAY Bestselling Author

JANICE KAY JOHNSON

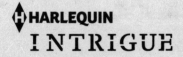

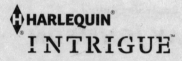

ISBN-13: 978-1-335-48948-7

Mustang Creek Manhunt

Copyright © 2022 by Janice Kay Johnson

Harlequin Enterprises ULC
22 Adelaide St. West, 41st Floor
Toronto, Ontario M5H 4E3, Canada
www.Harlequin.com

Printed in U.S.A.

An author of more than ninety books for children and adults with more than seventy-five for Harlequin, **Janice Kay Johnson** writes about love and family and pens books of gripping romantic suspense. A *USA TODAY* bestselling author and an eight-time finalist for the Romance Writers of America RITA® Award, she won a RITA® Award in 2008. A former librarian, Janice raised two daughters in a small town north of Seattle, Washington.

Books by Janice Kay Johnson

Harlequin Intrigue

Hide the Child
Trusting the Sheriff
Within Range
Brace for Impact
The Hunting Season
The Last Resort
Cold Case Flashbacks
Dead in the Water
Mustang Creek Manhunt

Visit the Author Profile page at Harlequin.com.

CAST OF CHARACTERS

Melinda McIntosh—Childhood trauma makes trust hard for Melinda, a police detective. She let down her guard once for a man, but never again. Now she can't let her hostility prevent her from working with the same man to take down a serial rapist determined to take revenge on everyone responsible for his downfall.

Boyd Chaney—Former army ranger, now cattle rancher and county sheriff, Boyd fell in love with a woman determined to risk her life. He couldn't handle that again—but everything changes now as they hunt a monster who is killing cops and hates Melinda McIntosh most of all.

Gene Dorrance—He knows who to blame for the raid that destroyed his twisted life. After seven long years in prison, he's pardoned—and free to begin his vicious quest.

Daniel Deperro—A detective who works with Melinda, Daniel leads the hunt for Dorrance. He doesn't expect his precious adopted daughter, five-year-old Chloe, to be endangered.

Kristina Morgan—A nurse at the local hospital, she once foolishly befriended a patient. As payback, he'll take everything she has to give.

Chapter One

A Boyd Chaney sighting, whether in-person or courtesy of news media, could sour any day for Melinda McIntosh. Unfortunately, those sightings had become increasingly common since he'd been elected Granger County sheriff. This morning was a perfect example. There she'd been, happily prepared to dig into her breakfast cereal, when she spread her morning newspaper on the kitchen table only to see a large photo of him, front page and above the fold.

Of course *he* wouldn't be relegated to page four. After winning the election, he'd apparently designated himself spokesperson for the sheriff's department. Local journalists ate up his every all-knowing pronouncement. Half the time, he was on the air or in the newspaper expressing opinions about other events that had taken place in this rural eastern Oregon county. Or maybe they latched on to him because he managed to look dauntingly authoritative, not to mention tall, lean and broad-shouldered, every inch the decorated former army ranger he was. Reassuring. Even his heavy-lidded eyes and almost smile came across as sexy without diminishing his air of comptence.

The voters had cast their ballots for him because, although he'd only been resident in the county for something like five years and had zero background in law enforcement, he co-owned the biggest horse and cattle ranch in these parts and had served his country overseas. He wore the dark green, sheriff's department Stetson as if he'd been born to it.

Melinda realized her hands had tightened convulsively on the steering wheel of her squad car until her knuckles ached. She was driving back toward Sadler after conducting an interview, but she'd tuned out radio traffic, and there had been some. She knew better than to let herself brood while she was on the job! *Okay, deep breath. In, out. Relax.* It could be worse. At least she hadn't seen him in person recently, and the last time had only been a glimpse when—

Her gaze focused on a black car shooting toward her in the oncoming lane on the highway. Damn, it was moving fast, almost blurring before her eyes. Not usually her business—out here beyond the city limits, she had no jurisdiction. If she'd spotted someone going ten to twenty miles over the speed limit, she'd have let them go.

This kind of driving wasn't something she could ignore.

She braked and steered to the shoulder, the right tires crunching on gravel, and was reaching for the radio when the car blew by. Two men. She thought heads turned, although it was barely a quick impression. They had to have made her vehicle as law enforcement even though it was unmarked.

She performed a U-turn and accelerated after the car, stunned by how far behind she'd already fallen. The other driver had to be going a hundred miles an hour.

Melinda identified herself to dispatch, gave her approximate location and reported, "In pursuit of a black sedan, dull matte finish. The license plate is in-state, but I couldn't get the number. Are any units in place to intercept?"

Other voices responded. One sheriff's deputy was on a paved crossroad about twenty miles to the north and was turning around to reach the highway. An Oregon state patrolman was the best bet—if the speeding car stayed on this highway.

She accelerated to a speed she'd never before attempted. If the highway had been busier, she wouldn't have dared; high-speed pursuits were discouraged for good reason. Better to set up a roadblock or even let the speeder go than be responsible for a hideous multivehicle accident involving civilians.

A voice she recognized but wouldn't expect to hear under these circumstances came on. Head of the investigative division within the Sadler Police Department, Lieutenant Edward Matson was her boss. He sounded tense.

"The Wells Fargo bank in town was just robbed. Witness descriptions of the vehicle in which the two robbers fled matches what you saw, Detective Mc-

Intosh. Dull, overall black paint job. We don't have a make and model."

"I saw two men," she said. "Didn't get a good look given the speed they were traveling."

And wouldn't you know, that was the moment when another man jumped into the discussion: Sheriff Boyd Chaney himself. Of course, his voice was deep and steady. It always was. His unrelenting control was both admirable and irritating.

"Do *not* make an individual stop," he ordered. "If the vehicle should pull over, wait for backup."

Her temper flared at the idea he thought he could tell her what to do, but this time she couldn't dispute his logic, or his right to make the decisions. This *was* his jurisdiction. Plus she assumed he wasn't speaking only to her.

"Acknowledged," the deputy agreed.

She echoed him, if a little stiffly, as did the state trooper.

"Do you still have a visual, Detective?" Chaney asked.

"Barely," Melinda admitted. "You know that Y is up ahead. I'm hoping to see which way the car goes."

"I'm now on State Route 23 waiting to intercept," he continued calmly.

He must have been monitoring the radio from his home on his large ranch. All he'd have had to do was drive out to the main road, which was the likeliest choice for fleeing bank robbers to choose. It would carry them to Highway 97, eastern Oregon's major north-south throughway. Unless they had a local bolt-hole...

If that was true, they must be panicking about now. If Melinda could see them, they could see her. If they'd imagined they could get out of Sadler, the county seat, fast enough to turn off on some dirt road to a rural property, they knew by now that the plan was in jeopardy. Boyd wasn't the man to let them race on by. If he was alone, what would he do? Shoot out the tires and precipitate a screeching, rolling, probably deadly "accident"? Or did he have one or more of his fellow retired army rangers accompanying him so they could set up a roadblock? Melinda had reason to know that Gabe Decker, the ranch co-owner, was stunningly skilled both with weapons and behind the wheel of a car. The ranch foreman, Leon Cabrera, had been a sharpshooter during his army deployments.

Yeah, but they'd end up in big trouble for getting involved in a police operation.

Despite everything going on in her head, she stayed conscious of continuing chatter from the radio. The deputy was in place if the vehicle decided on Option #2, while the state trooper drew closer from the north. A second sheriff's deputy was joining the pursuit, but coming from well behind Melinda so not likely to be of any use.

Other state troopers had chimed in too, all prepared to watch for the car she'd described if the handful of officers closing in failed to make the stop.

Chaney asked Lieutenant Matson what weapons the

bank robbers had displayed. The news wasn't good. They'd brandished both semiautomatic handguns and an assault rifle. Melinda didn't like the growing fear she felt for her nemesis, Boyd Chaney, the likeliest of them all to put himself on the line. Naturally, if *he* felt any anxiety, she couldn't hear it in his voice, which suggested he'd faced plenty of situations as ugly and emerged unscathed. Which was probably true.

Except, there'd been one time he hadn't, she knew. He'd left the army rangers after suffering catastrophic injuries that left him unable to return to active duty. To her deep regret, she'd seen his scars and the rest of his long, muscled body, too.

Had he forgotten that he was breakable, like ordinary people? Melinda asked herself in frustration.

The wail of her siren was a weird accompaniment as she kept the gas pedal to the floor. She couldn't have done it if this part of the county weren't so flat that many roads were almost ruler straight. She'd see any approaching traffic from a long distance away, too. The worst immediate disaster would be having wildlife dash right in front of her, always a possibility. Mule deer or a herd of fleet-footed pronghorns were the likeliest. Or a ranch vehicle making a slow turn onto the highway from a dirt driveway.

Although at least that would raise a cloud of dust and be moving slowly enough she could probably swerve around it without any difficulty.

"I'm gaining ground," she reported tensely. "I don't think they're slowing." Her SUV, built for law enforcement, had a more powerful engine than just about anything else on the road.

Chaney again. "A southbound semitruck just passed."

There was taut silence until she was able to report that first the speeding car and then her vehicle had flown safely past the semi. The relief went unspoken because it was so premature.

And then, "Sheriff, he's coming your way," Melinda said.

The deputy's voice crackled over the airwaves. "I'll join you."

"I think I see him," Chaney said suddenly. He must be using binoculars.

Oh, God.

"What's the plan?" she asked.

A different voice—the state trooper—said, "It just came in sight for me, too. We might be able to set up a roadblock."

"Going that fast, he could blast right through us," Chaney said. And yes, he probably knew plenty about roadblocks and both defensive and offensive driving. "Why don't you turn around? I'll pull out onto the highway right in behind him and hit the lights and siren. You can join me. Deputy Heaton, if you're ready, we'll close around him."

"You watch out," the state trooper said.

"Will do. Detective, I don't know if you can join us in time—"

She'd known that was coming. He didn't like

women in law enforcement. Or maybe it was just *her* being a cop.

"The more of us there, the better."

The deputy would be bursting out of the crossroad any minute. If they could surround the speeding car, overwhelm it with their presence, they might have a chance to make the arrests without a gun battle. It was rare for bank robbers to actually kill anyone, she'd learned from her training. But these two, who knew how they'd react to stress?

DAMN, BOYD HATED that Melinda, of all people, was involved. She was a good cop, he *knew* she was, but if he had to see her shot, he didn't know how he could live with it. If they shot her, he knew damn well he wouldn't be arresting and cuffing those two with the professionalism required by a man in his job.

He also wished he and the others weren't planning a difficult move conducted at a high speed when the four of them had never worked together. His own deputy was his biggest concern; when Boyd had taken over the sheriff's department, he'd found an appalling lack of training and support. He could at least assume the trooper had been trained in these kinds of maneuvers.

Here came the black bullet. Attention split between his rearview mirror and the view ahead, he accelerated on the shoulder, determined to reach maximum speed to enable him to pull in tight behind the target. Hard to judge, but—

He looked the passenger right in the eye as the

car passed and then tucked his police SUV in behind, dangerously close to the bumper in front of him. Within moments, Heaton exploded out onto the highway to close in on the driver's side. The trooper, who'd also built up speed on the shoulder, squeezed in on the right, and within minutes Melinda's unit joined Boyd to complete a pincer movement. All four of them had lights flashing and sirens screaming. Pray to God no southbound traffic appeared right now. Boyd watched for any sign those fools were going to start shooting, but after a minute brake lights flashed and the black car began slowing.

Their speed dropped to eighty, seventy, a more sane sixty miles per hour. Still no other approaching traffic. Boyd didn't take his eyes off what he could see of the two men in the vehicle ahead of him.

At his order, Heaton pulled up so he was even with the front fender of the speeding car as he gestured for it to pull over. The state trooper sped a distance ahead before swerving to block the northbound lane. He immediately leaped out and planted himself behind the bulk of his vehicle with a rifle braced to open fire.

Within moments, the car pulled onto the shoulder and came to a stop, squeezed on three sides. Heaton was out, crouched behind his vehicle, handgun held in a two-fisted grip. Melinda followed suit, staying behind her car door.

This was the most dangerous moment.

Boyd grabbed a microphone, opened his door and called, "Step out of your vehicle. *Now.* Hands up, in plain sight."

The pause seemed excruciatingly long, but probably didn't last fifteen seconds. First the driver-side door opened, then the passenger side. Boyd didn't take anything for granted until both men were lying on the pavement, cuffed and had been searched. They had guns aplenty in the car, but had been smart enough to know when to give up.

Even then, the fear that clutched Boyd's belly hadn't loosened its grip. Sweat soaked his uniform shirt beneath his arms and down his spine. He hadn't felt anything like this since his first few combat experiences in Iraq, and he knew who to blame.

Tall and slender, Melinda stood not five feet from him, her Glock held steady in her hands as she stared down at the two men who both had their heads turned away from her. Eyes that could look as richly colored as a forest glade were steely, her mouth tight.

"Let's load them," she said.

Boyd pried his clenched jaws apart enough to allow him to say, "Would you prefer to stay with the car? We can transport the prisoners for you."

Her eyes held deep suspicion. "No, I'll take one. If I can borrow Deputy Heaton to take the other, I'd appreciate that. I would prefer to keep them separated."

He bent his head in acquiescence, his neck stiff.

She hadn't been willing to give him a break, not *one*, since he'd screwed up so badly with her. He had to accept that she was a cop, a good one from what he'd seen and heard, but he hated the idea of her driving that many miles with one of these potentially violent scumbags sitting in the back of her car, filled with hate as he stared at her through the grille.

Not my business.

The state trooper cleared his throat. "I'll get on the radio and let everyone know we've wound up this incident successfully. Then I'd better get back on the road myself."

Boyd wrenched his gaze from Melinda's and held out his hand to the trooper. "Thanks. Wouldn't have gone nearly as well without you."

The guy, tall and lean, probably in his forties, grinned as he shook Boyd's hand. "Sheriff." He nodded at Heaton and Melinda. "Deputy. Ma'am."

Boyd waited for her to snap, *I'm a detective, not a ma'am*, but she smiled. "It was a pleasure." Apparently, she saved all her aggravation for him.

"Let's load 'em," Boyd growled, and bent to pull the driver to his feet.

Head down and unresisting, the bank robber stumbled to Heaton's squad car and climbed in with minimal assistance. Boyd slammed the door behind him and turned to find that Heaton and Melinda had the other prisoner up.

Tight-lipped, Boyd jerked his head toward her vehicle. "I'll wait here for a photographer and the tow truck. I assume you'll want the car delivered to your city impound?"

Still obviously wary, she said, "Yes. Thank you. I'll make the call."

Maybe he'd regain his equilibrium before the police photographer arrived. "Drive carefully."

Melinda nodded in his direction, spoke briefly to Heaton, got into her squad car and drove away without another word to Boyd. Not even a glance back in her rearview mirror, as far as he could tell.

Left alone on the side of the highway with his stomach roiling and his rib cage feeling tight, all Boyd could think was that he and Melinda had never had a chance. Given hindsight, he couldn't imagine why he'd ever dreamed they could sustain even a short-term relationship.

But she looked as enticing as ever, and a hard truth stirred the turmoil beneath his breastbone. He still wanted this woman as much as ever, even if he couldn't see himself breaking his vow.

He would never again let himself care too much about a woman who regularly put her life on the line, no matter how sexist that made him look.

As she drove, Melinda kept an eye on her prisoner, who hung his head and averted his gaze. Didn't say a word.

That left her free to kick her own ass for bristling the way she had at the least excuse. Really? She'd promised herself to be cool and completely professional the next time she and Boyd happened to encounter each other. She could only hope he hadn't noticed how she reacted to him. He hadn't done or said anything to set her off. Her mistake had been letting her guard down for him in the first place. She wished she'd never let him see the vulnerability she normally covered effectively behind her kick-ass cop persona. Which—face it—was who'd she'd become. The gut-wrenching end to her relationship with Boyd Chaney had been the final punctuation. Balancing a relationship or family and the job wasn't happening, not for her. She couldn't even let herself regret that.

Next time she had to deal with him—and there would be a next time—she'd do better.

And—damn—she'd just driven most of the way back to Sadler while, once again, allowing herself to be oblivious to other traffic and exchanges on the radio. She'd get herself or someone else killed if she couldn't keep her focus when she was on the job.

A few turns in town and she pulled in behind the jail, parking right beside Deputy Heaton's squad car. A cluster of cops and guards had been waiting for them. Three peeled off to take charge of her prisoner.

She got out and greeted them, not surprised to see that a fellow detective, Sergeant Daniel Deperro, was first to reach her. As the most experienced investigator in their department, he was something of a mentor to her. Matson had started talking about retiring, and everyone assumed that Daniel would be promoted to take his place. Melinda hoped that happened. Daniel, too, had seen plenty of active duty in the military, but unlike Chaney he never treated her any differently than he did the male members of their unit. He'd never shown any interest in her as a woman, either, but these days she was grateful for that. Respect and friendship were what mattered.

She wouldn't diminish herself for any man, and that's what she'd felt Boyd Chaney had asked of her.

Chapter Two

While she ate her lunch in the break room at the police station—leftover vegetarian chili reheated in the microwave—Melinda idly read the *Oregonian* newspaper, one of the West Coast's major dailies. This was a two-day-old edition she'd somehow missed. Bite halfway to her mouth, she lost interest in food as her gaze snapped to a headline: *Outgoing governor pardons convicted killers*.

What? Okay, it wasn't uncommon for a governor to issue some pardons on his or her way out the door. Convicts on the list might be elderly and a burden on the taxpayers, or people convicted of murders that were so personal—say, a woman who'd killed an abusive husband—they were unlikely to reoffend. Or there could well be cases where there was serious reason to question the conviction.

She was being paranoid, that's all. She'd checked on Gene Dorrance not that long ago—a couple of months, maybe?—and he'd still been in lockup at the state penitentiary in Salem in western Oregon. He hadn't been convicted of murder or even manslaughter, but even so, if he'd come up for parole, her department should have been notified so an arresting officer could attend the hearing. The threats he'd made as he'd shuffled, shackled at wrists and ankles, out of the courtroom were on record.

Still, appetite abandoning her, she set the spoon back in the bowl and kept reading, apprehensive despite herself. She never had liked the current governor; since he was being tossed out after one term, clearly the majority of voters felt the same.

She had to turn pages and refold the newspaper to continue reading the article. Now she was just scanning, looking for familiar names.

A familiar name.

It wouldn't be here. Nobody was crazy enough to let—

The name jumped out at her. *Gene Dorrance*. Melinda sat staring down at it. For how long, she didn't know, but her lungs suddenly demanded air. Her mouth must have been hanging open, too, because it was so dry she reached for her bottle of water.

And then she read the brief paragraph about the man who'd kidnapped and held two young women—one a minor—for over two years, sexually molesting them the entire time.

Melinda would see those faces in her mind's eye until her dying day. Gaunt, expressionless, eyes dulled by lack of hope. Racks of bone, their entire bodies showing years of suffering. Rescuers had had to speak to the women quietly, gently; they seemed confused by any directions, unresponsive. Melinda remembered the photos of two other young women who'd been reported missing in the same period. Neither were found at his place, but she was almost positive that at least one of them had been there. His two captives had, after a period of hospitalization, both mentioned hearing whimpering when he first dragged them into his basement.

The article didn't say why the governor would have chosen to pardon this monster, or who had recommended Dorrance for his consideration. Melinda started to reach for her phone, intending to call a guy who worked in the warden's office at the prison whom she'd gotten to know in the past, but then she thought better of it. Front section of the newspaper crushed in her hand, she left the break room, cut through the detective squad room and reached Lieutenant Matson's office. The door stood partly ajar, but she rapped on it and waited for his voice.

"I'm here."

She marched in and laid the paper in front of him. "Did you know about this?"

"This?" He was already reading. After a moment, he shoved back his chair and shot to his feet. "Of course I didn't know! Why the hell weren't we notified?"

"Because he wasn't paroled. But *this*—" She felt sick. "They still should have let us know. What were they thinking?"

He shook his head. Matson had been primary on the investigation, as horrified as she'd been. Melinda had been a patrol officer at the time. After speaking to Dorrance as a responding officer, but unable to substantiate the information in a 911 call about potential domestic violence, she'd been left with a bad feeling. A *really* bad feeling. She'd seen a couple of small things that conflicted with what Dorrance had told her. She'd gone to the lieutenant, who listened to her. Somehow, Dorrance had learned about her role in bringing him down. She'd become the focus of his greatest rage. Probably, she'd thought at the time, because he couldn't endure the idea of being bested by a woman.

Matson was already in the middle of making a call. She plopped down on a chair and waited. As angry as the lieutenant was, eavesdropping was easy.

"He was released *two days ago*?" Matson hardly ever raised his voice, but this was an exception. He'd all but rattled the glass in the window inset in the door. "Nobody paid attention to the notation that this convict's last words in the courtroom were a promise to take revenge on everyone who'd had anything to do with his arrest? And those two women—" His eyes met Melinda's. "We need to locate them immediately. I'm guessing they haven't been warned, either?"

His expression became grimmer by the minute. He didn't like anything he was hearing. Yet when he ended the call, he set down his phone almost gently. As if the alternative had been slamming it down hard enough to break it.

"Dorrance was a good boy. With no infractions on his record while he was in custody. The attempt prison officials made to throw cold water on this plan was ignored. And no, they have no idea where Dorrance is. He walked out a free man. Wasn't required to give an address or even the name of a contact."

"He's here," she said numbly. "You know he is."

"It's been, what, seven years? That first rage might have dissipated."

"He's vicious and crazy. What, you think he got rehabilitated?"

Her boss groaned, scraped a hand over his face and sank back down on his desk chair. "No. I think he's spent those seven years making detailed plans. Lovingly revising them."

"We need to inform every single person he might blame. And then we have to find Dorrance."

"I agree. Is Deperro here?"

"He was at his desk a minute ago." Melinda frowned. "He wasn't with the department back then."

"No, but he's best qualified to lead any manhunt we launch."

Her mouth opened, but Matson shook his head.

"He has experience you don't, but no matter what, paying *you* back is that madman's number one objective. We can't put you out there leading this operation."

Fear drove some of her fury. "You expect me to hide in my closet? Take a vacation? Waste more time on the question of whether we should arrest a kid for borrowing his daddy's car?"

The lieutenant winced. "You're still on that?"

"Yeah." She was all but quivering with intensity. "Along with trying to figure out who's smashing car windows at the mall so they can help themselves to whatever shoppers left in open invitation on the front seat."

He grimaced. "I'm not saying you can't be involved with this hunt. We'd never have caught him if it weren't for you. You had more insight then into who he really was than the rest of us put together. We'll need you to predict his moves. I just can't have you on public display."

What could she do but give a tight nod? She tended to get prickly when her ability to do the job was discounted, and with good reason, but in this case she did understand his decision.

"Stick your head out and call Deperro in here," he added. "Warnings to any conceivable targets have to come first."

BY THE TIME Daniel Deperro got off the call he'd been on and joined Matson and Melinda in the small office, the lieutenant had pulled up the bare-bones records.

"I don't want to miss anybody," he said. "Melinda, why don't you call Records and get them to send up everything we stored?"

Binders and boxes filled with police reports, evidence ranging from bloody garments to guns and plaster casts of footprints or tire prints, interview transcripts, photographs and more were stored in the basement. Recently, the records department had needed to expand into the basement of city hall. What she'd be requesting should still be stored in this building, though.

Melinda stepped out of the office to make that call

while Matson shared Gene Dorrance's history with Deperro, explaining why they believed he'd follow through with his threats.

The lieutenant's decision to put Daniel Deperro in charge might have stung more, except Melinda respected her fellow detective and liked him. Too many cops in this conservative, rural county still didn't want to work with women. She'd had to fight hard to get where she was. Daniel had never once treated her as anything but a smart cop deservedly promoted to the detective squad. Off the job, she'd become good friends with him and his social worker wife, Lindsay. Just last weekend, she'd gone riding with them both at Daniel's small ranch, where he bred and trained quarter horses for fun.

Reentering the office, she said, "They promised to have everything up here in fifteen minutes max."

"Good," Matson said grimly. "I say we find the two women before we do anything else."

"They need to go into hiding," Daniel agreed.

Melinda had grabbed her laptop, but didn't immediately start a search. "I had a thought."

Both men waited.

"I think we should go to the press. TV, newspapers, even local bloggers. Get his face out there. Identify him as dangerous and likely armed. Ask anyone who sees him to contact us immediately."

Cops in general dodged reporters whenever they could, so she wasn't surprised that Lieutenant Matson and Daniel stared at her in appalled silence for a minute.

Daniel was the first to nod, although he didn't look happy. "Much as I hate the idea of creating community-wide hysteria, I agree. Spreading his picture as widely as we can is the best way to hinder his movements. And as far as we know, he's not an experienced killer."

"I've always believed he is," Melinda said. She told him that the two women they'd rescued had insisted there'd been a third women in the home initially. "But it's more than that. The guy is forty-seven years old. Forty when he was convicted. These two victims were supposed to be the first he ever abducted and raped? I seriously doubt that. There could have been a long succession of them. We just didn't find the graves."

"It's also possible these were the first he kept around for a long time," Matson suggested, not for the first time. They'd had this discussion before. "He could have warmed up to it with one-time rapes and, yeah, possibly murder."

"None of the work on his house that created the lockdowns where he imprisoned the women looked recent."

Matson didn't remind her that Dorrance had held both women long enough to give the additional walls, doors and locks time to age. Melinda knew that, but she'd all but swear she'd seen a cluster of ghosts down in that basement. Or at least felt icy shivers from them breathing down her neck. Of course, she'd never told anyone that, and wouldn't now. It didn't matter, anyway; what mattered was protecting everyone Dorrance had threatened and throwing him back behind bars for the rest of his life if he made a move on anyone.

She, her lieutenant and Daniel divided up initial tasks. Matson would make immediate contact with everyone who had prosecuted Dorrance—and with the defense team, in case he was angry because his lawyers had failed to get him off. The lieutenant would also talk to the Sadler PD chief, who liked to be kept up-to-date and would need to warn the mayor before the press conference.

Daniel was to sit down with the evidence boxes, familiarizing himself with the investigation, and while he was at it, make a list of every person who'd been involved, in case Matson and Melinda had forgotten someone. He intended to search for any links Dorrance had with anyone—family or friend—who might be close enough to offer him shelter now.

Melinda was to locate and warn the two female victims, then every cop who'd had anything to do with the investigation and arrest.

"The neighbor who called 911 in the first place," she said. "If she hasn't moved…"

"Put her on the list," the lieutenant agreed.

She opened her laptop as soon as she sat down at her desk. She'd kept track of the two victims for a couple of years, but, unsurprisingly, neither wanted to stay in the area.

"If I dare go out in public, every single person who sees me will know exactly what happened to me," one of them had told Melinda. "That's all they'll see. I want a chance to not be pitiful in everyone's eyes."

Melinda had been impressed by Andrea Kudelka's strength, once she'd had a few weeks to start believing her ordeal really was over. Her eyes remained haunted, though, and anything an outsider would call real recovery was certainly years away, if it ever happened.

The two had shown no inclination to cling to each other. To the contrary. Until the rescue, they had never met face-to-face, knew each other only from screams and sobs muffled by thick cinder-block walls.

"Seeing her reminds me of what happened," Erica Warner had told Melinda in a whisper.

Her own attempt to stay in touch with both women had quickly ended. *She* reminded them of the horror they'd lived through, too.

Andrea had been a local girl living on her own, even though her parents were still resident in Sadler. Erica was from… Eugene, on the other side of the state, if Melinda remembered right. She'd been a horse-crazy kid who had been thrilled to get a job on a dude ranch. Initially, at least, she'd gone home to Eugene, but chances were everyone she'd known there had also pored over every detail made public of her hideous experience, and she'd face exactly what Andrea had already foreseen.

In fact, as Melinda began her search, it was apparent Erica's parents no longer lived in Eugene. The

Kudelkas had moved away as well, but an aunt Melinda remembered seeing was still listed locally.

The question was, would their captor want to punish them for their escape before he did anything else, or would his greatest need be revenge against the people who had destroyed his life?

With a groan, she picked up her phone. Police officers first; she could reach them, or at least most of them, a lot more quickly than she could trace two women who had been determined to disappear.

As, she hoped, had the next-door neighbor, whose name was no longer listed by the phone company.

BOYD LAY ON his belly in the dirt, eye to the Leupold tactical scope attached to his Remington M24 rifle. Keeping his sniper skills sharp was probably a waste of time these days, but the attack made on the ranch a couple of years ago had convinced him that no place was safe. Besides, he liked the precision, the intense concentration he had to summon to shoot accurately over several hundred yards.

He might not have bothered building a gun range here on ranch land had it been only for him, but his partner and the ranch co-owner, Gabe Decker, was also a retired army ranger, as was their foreman, Leon Cabrera. Leon was one of the best snipers Boyd had ever seen work.

He and Gabe liked hiring former rangers, or at least giving refuge to men who needed to reintegrate into society and weren't doing so well at it. The range

gave them all a chance to decompress while also reminding them of things they'd done well.

Yeah, is that what I'm doing out here today? Boyd
asked himself. *Trying to convince myself I know what
the hell I'm doing with my life?*

He wished he had an answer.

Wiping his mind clean, slowing his breathing, he
gently pulled the trigger. Once, twice, three times,
before he paused to study the target. Those had been
damn good shots, would have been kill shots at five
hundred yards. He still had it—whatever *it* was.

But, damn, there were things he should be doing
instead of coming out here to the range by himself.
Gabe was having to shoulder too much responsibility for ranch operations since Boyd had taken on a
second job: county sheriff. Trouble was, this was
home for the two men now, both of whom had been
badly enough injured, they'd had to leave the army
sooner than they'd planned. It hadn't taken long for
Boyd, who settled here in Oregon first, to discover
how incompetent the sheriff was and, therefore, how
useless it was to call for any help from law enforcement. He'd been mad enough to decide he could do
better, even if he'd never been a cop before.

Now he had to prove it, which meant he had two
full-time-plus jobs.

Can't work 24/7, he told himself, grimacing as he
rose from his prone position. He'd damn near lost his
right leg, courtesy of an explosive that had flipped
his Humvee, and the scar tissue wasn't the only re-

minder. He hurt more when he was on his feet than when he was on horseback, Gabe the opposite.

His phone vibrated in his pocket, which didn't thrill him. What new screwup or even disaster would he now have to deal with?

The name on the screen stunned him. Melinda McIntosh. The last thing *she'd* ever want to do again was call him. This had to be bad.

He pressed his thumb to the "accept" button and answered. "Chaney here."

"Sheriff, do you have a minute?" she asked stiffly.

Sheriff? Really? They'd made love, spent one especially memorable night in his big bed here at the ranch. That lovemaking had been so good, he wondered if it could ever be near as good with any other woman. Which was a stupid damn thing to think, but this wasn't the first time it had crossed his mind.

Irritated, he said, "For you, I have a minute. *Melinda.*"

Silence shimmered in his ear before she conceded. "Boyd."

"What's up?"

"We have a situation. Ah, I need you to call one of your detectives, Miguel Cordova. You may know he was an SPD officer who shifted to working for the county when you had an opening for a detective."

Before Boyd had become sheriff, but he did vaguely know Cordova's work history. The guy was sharp, unlike several deputies Boyd had been nudging toward retirement or had already let go.

"I thought this would be better coming from you,"

she continued, "and we'd have needed to bring you up to speed anyway."

One-handed, he snapped his rifle case closed and slid it onto the back seat of his pickup, slammed the door then got in behind the wheel. He didn't make any move to start the engine.

Her tension was contagious.

"Up to speed on what?"

She summed it up quickly: seven years ago, Sadler PD had arrested a real creep who'd kidnapped two young women and held them for years so that he could rape them repeatedly. He—Gene Dorrance—had been convicted, no problem, and gone off for a long stay at the Oregon State Penitentiary.

"I was catching up while I ate lunch today by reading a two-day-old *Oregonian*."

Hell. He never missed a day's paper. This had to be connected to the article—

"The governor pardoned a whole bunch of inmates. One of them was Dorrance. By the time we called over to the prison today, he was long gone."

Having a really bad feeling about this, Boyd asked, "Why would he come back to Sadler?"

"I was in the courthouse when he was led out. Somehow, he spotted me. He was looking me right in the eye when he said, 'I'll pay you back. Every last one of you.'"

Boyd's eyes closed and he bumped his head against the headrest. "Were you the only arresting officer in the courtroom for the verdict?"

"No, several of us were there. Actually…" There

was the tiniest hesitation. "I wasn't a detective yet, and wasn't the arresting officer, but he blamed me most of all."

This was what he'd feared when he found himself falling for a woman with a dangerous job. It had been her choice, not his, to break off the relationship, but he'd convinced himself she'd made the best choice for both of them.

So why was he as scared as he could ever remember being?

Chapter Three

Sergeant Tom Alvarez walked around the corner of the single-story, ranch-style house to meet Melinda, who had peeked in what windows she could on the north side. Two bedrooms, clearly unused, while the blinds were closed tight on what was probably the master bedroom window. Fortunately, gates on each side of the house had made their first reconnoiter easy.

She felt lucky to have been able to pull the sergeant in instead of having to bring a green patrol officer. Deperro now had more important things to do this afternoon than provide her with backup while she verified that the one cop she hadn't been able to reach was fine. Fortunately, the alarm was being taken seriously department wide. She wasn't the only cop to have heard Dorrance's threat.

"Window into the garage is covered," Alvarez reported. "Can't tell if Guy's pickup is in there or not."

Guy Jonas hadn't been answering his phone. This…welfare check, yeah, that was the best way to describe it, was a product of her paranoia. He was probably fine. Jonas was off for two days, yesterday and today. Officers were encouraged to answer their phones even when they were off duty, but that wasn't a rule set in stone. Hard to grab a call if you were riding a cutting horse in a competition, climbing Mount Baker, or were head-deep in the engine of a car you were working on. Sometimes, you just needed to turn off the ringer and pretend the job didn't exist.

That said, Melinda had left two messages on Jonas's voice mail this afternoon. She'd have expected him to check it, whatever he was up to. When she was being fair, she'd describe him as conscientious on the job. He made it hard for her to like him, because he'd let her know in subtle and not-so-subtle ways since she hired on that he thought law enforcement should be a male-only profession. Of course, half the other officers with SPD probably thought the same. They'd just shrugged as time went on and resigned themselves to being stuck with her. She'd like to think she had won over some of those.

But not Jonas.

Which had nothing to do with the fact that she and Tom Alvarez were going to have to break into a fellow officer's house.

Back door, they decided. Their entry would be less obvious to neighbors, and the pane of glass inset in the kitchen door would be easier and cheaper to replace than a larger front window.

Peering in, Melinda hammered on the door again. Nothing moved. He'd left dirty dishes piled in the sink; from here, she couldn't tell whether they were breakfast or lunch dishes or left over from the evening before. The kitchen wasn't a pit, though. He must mop occasionally, and no food had been left out on the counter. He wasn't married, she knew. As with too many other cops, he had at least one divorce in his past.

Alvarez grimaced, pulled his service weapon and reversed it in his hand so he could use the butt to break the glass. "He's going to be mad as hell," he muttered. "Jonas isn't the understanding kind."

He did have friends in the department, Melinda knew, although apparently Tom Alvarez wasn't one of them. Maybe Jonas didn't like working with someone who had darker skin than his any more than he did women.

"Do it," she ordered.

Glass splintered and fell, most inside, some onto the coir mat at their feet. She half expected to hear a roar of anger, but it didn't come. Guy Jonas either wasn't home, or—

No. I'm being paranoid, she reminded herself. Why would Dorrance have started with Jonas, who along with her had been a first responder on that domestic violence call but had hung back and made his skepticism for her theories plain? Dorrance should have *thanked* him.

Alvarez used the butt to clear enough shards so that he could reach in and unlock the door. As he opened it, he called, "We're coming in, Guy! It's the police." He kept his Glock in his hand, but at his side. Startling a cop in his own home could be dangerous and he was clearly aiming to appear as unthreatening as possible while being ready in case anyone else was in the house.

Melinda unsnapped her holster and rested her hand on the butt of her police-issue Glock as she stepped inside.

Listening hard, she also drew in a deep breath, and swore.

Tom Alvarez did the same.

After a single glance at each other, not needing words, they did a seamless sweep of the house. The smell of death didn't mean someone who was still alive couldn't still be in here.

They found Jonas sprawled on the carpeted floor right beside the bed in his room. A horrifying amount of blood had soaked into the carpet around his head and shoulders, much of it drying now. This hadn't just happened. He'd either grabbed for the bedside stand on his way down and pulled it over, or it got knocked over in a struggle. A lamp had hit the floor, the bulb breaking. The drawer was half open, a few items spilling out, including a small box of condoms.

Melinda felt a pang of pity for him. There'd be no dignity in this death. He'd have zero privacy left once the crime scene team had gone over his house and the ME took his body.

Emotions sharp—the victims of violence she saw in the course of her job were rarely anyone she knew—she still studied his position, facedown on the floor.

Without flipping him over, her best guess was that his killer had yanked back his head and sliced his throat. Jonas was—had been—on the tall side, but thin. Dorrance…wasn't as big a man as Daniel Deperro or Boyd Chaney, but tall enough and muscular besides. She wondered if he'd taken up weight lifting while he served his time. That would make sense, given his goals.

"Would Guy have had a gun safe?" She speculated aloud.

Alvarez tore his gaze from the dead man and turned his head to scan the room. "I doubt it. Lived alone, no kids. He was pretty cocky. Wouldn't have seen any need for one." His eyes settled on the drawer spilling its contents. Which did *not* include a handgun.

"He was going for his gun," Melinda said slowly.

The sergeant didn't disagree. "Ten more seconds, he might have reached it in time."

"If we're right, Dorrance just armed himself."

"Yeah. Hell."

"I don't see a phone, either. You'd think it would be here by the bed."

"It's got to be locked. Dorrance wasn't any kind of digital whiz, was he?"

"I don't think so. He was an auto mechanic." Which involved a lot more electronics than it used to. She frowned. "We can't close our mind to other possibilities. This could have nothing to do with Gene Dorrance."

"You're right," agreed the stocky cop at her side. "The timing, though…"

She let out a long breath and backed out of the

room. She wouldn't quit seeing this scene any time soon, and not even a shower and change of clothes would get rid of the stench, but she blanked her mind to it, took out her phone and called Deperro.

"He's dead," she said flatly. "I could be wrong, but it didn't just happen. I'm thinking last night. He's barefoot, wearing sweatpants and a white T-shirt." Well, it had started out white.

She told him the rest of their guesses. Daniel said he'd call CSI and would be out to the house to see the scene for himself. He'd let Lieutenant Matson know, too.

However reluctant she felt, Melinda knew she should call Boyd as well. The sheriff's department would be fully involved in the upcoming manhunt, and they had to keep him informed. She wasn't coward enough to ask someone else to be Boyd's contact.

"I'll go outside to make more calls," she told Alvarez.

He nodded. "Nothing more we can do right now." More softly, he said, "Why Jonas?"

"I don't know. He was an easy target, maybe. Living alone."

As she did, she couldn't help thinking. And how many others among the potential targets?

I've got to find those women.

BOYD DROVE FASTER than was justified to go look at a body that wouldn't be getting up and walking away any time soon. The patrol schedule he'd been working on could wait, though, and he felt an uncomfortable need to see Melinda. If she was upset, she'd hide it; he knew that, but there'd been something in her voice.

The victim was a man she'd known for years, had worked with. Boyd didn't like remembering the faces of men and sometimes boys he'd killed while he fought for his country's goals, but his nightmares usually centered on friends and members of his unit he'd seen go down.

Most of the city of Sadler, the county seat, was laid out logically enough he had no trouble finding the address. The house was a modest rambler with a sunbaked lawn, what might be a fruit tree in the backyard, but no flower beds or other evidence that the homeowner had been domestically inclined.

Boyd didn't recall meeting Guy Jonas, not a surprise since he only rarely had occasion to interact with rank-and-file SPD officers. All Melinda had said, quietly, was, "Jonas was a responder during our first contact with Dorrance. Not anyone I'd have expected Dorrance to start with." She'd hastened to add that they were looking at other angles, too, in case Jonas had made an enemy closer to home.

A crime scene van barricaded the driveway, and three police cars, marked and unmarked, crowded the curb. He parked half a block down and walked, keeping a sharp eye out around him. Was this Dorrance the kind to enjoy watching after the fact, savoring the uproar he'd stirred with the murder? Not much of anywhere to hide in this neighborhood, though, Boyd concluded. Most people were probably at work, so law enforcement vehicles were the only ones parked at the curb or in a driveway. Down at the corner, an older car sat on concrete blocks on a weedy strip next to a driveway, but Boyd had driven past it and was confident it wouldn't provide adequate cover for anyone to hide. Breaking into one of the houses and watching out the window would be a possibility, although he watched for movement and didn't see any.

Even so, he had a crawling sensation on the back of his neck, one he'd learned to heed. He'd thought he was done with this kind of tension when he moved to Oregon to raise cattle and horses, but no, he'd just had to throw his hat in the ring to run for sheriff.

Following the sound of voices, he walked around the side of the house and through a gate in the fence that stood open. Three people clustered on the concrete patio that otherwise held a grill and a picnic table. Boyd knew them all: Lieutenant Edward Matson, Detective Sergeant Daniel Deperro and Melinda. She wore what he'd learned was her usual plainclothes garb: black pants and a formfitting, crisp white button-up shirt. She added a blazer when temperatures dropped.

He wondered if she had any idea how damn sexy she was in that outfit. Somehow, it emphasized the length of her slim legs and the subtle curves of her lithe body. Even her hairstyle, captured in a knot at her nape, only succeeded in emphasizing the fine bone structure of her face.

Melinda saw him first. Her chin came up, probably in reaction to whatever she'd seen on his face, and she met his eyes almost defiantly.

He paused to say, "Mind if I take a look?" Hearing no objection, he went into the house, taking a moment to sign a sheet of paper someone had laid out on the kitchen counter as a log of who had entered the premises. He needed to get a grip on himself before he rejoined her and the other detectives.

A photographer seemed to be on his way out, but a couple of white-suited people crouched beside the body. CSI, he assumed, and a woman he recognized from the medical examiner's office.

She glanced up. "Ugly one."

"So I see."

To appearances, the victim hadn't gone to bed yet, but might have been on his way. Coming from the bathroom when he heard an unexpected sound and, instead of confronting an intruder unarmed, leaped for the drawer where he kept his sidearm? Mostly satisfied by that scenario, Boyd backed away.

He wished he'd asked about the phone. They would have looked for it, wouldn't they? Dumb question; all three of them had him beat where experience on major crimes investigations went.

The house only had one bathroom, and using his elbow he bumped the half-open door wide so he could take a look. A toothbrush sat in a glass to one side of the sink, but Jonas was tidy enough by habit to have put away the toothpaste. There were no obvious signs he'd just walked out of the bathroom before he met his death. Boyd didn't suppose it mattered, although he preferred to be able to envision a victim's last minutes.

He took a quick look around the house, but mostly what he saw were the usual indications that only one person lived here. One toothbrush, for starters. Recliner in front of the TV, remote right at hand, one chair half pulled out from the small table in the kitchen. Unused rooms. Much of the living room seemed unused, too, as if Jonas went straight to his recliner then followed the same path out when he was ready for bed. Yeah, the carpet showed wear on that path.

Outside, Boyd joined the three others. "Tell me about Jonas."

Matson and Daniel did most of the talking. Guy Jonas was forty-two years old, had been a cop for almost twenty of those years. He'd applied twice for openings on the detective squad, but hadn't been selected either time.

The lieutenant hesitated. "I won't say he wasn't a solid officer, but he was also rigid and set in his beliefs. He was furious when Detective McIntosh was promoted to one of those openings instead of him."

Melinda didn't give away any reaction at all.

Boyd looked at her. "You have any run-ins with him?"

Now her eyes narrowed. "You think *I* killed him because he was an intolerant jackass?"

"No." He let her see his impatience. "Just looking for a picture. You all knew him, I didn't."

"No run-ins. Just snide remarks, and sometimes

I'd turn my head and find him staring at me. There was something in his expression." She shook herself, or was that a shiver?

Daniel spoke up. "During the killing spree that involved Child Protective Services, I brought Lindsay to work with me one day and stowed her in the break room. I saw Jonas head in there and followed. He was expressing his opinion that the victims had all been scum who deserved what they got, and Lindsay said he'd stood there staring at her for a few minutes before he started sharing his opinion. Gave her the creeps, she said."

Melinda nodded. "She and I talked about it. I don't think Guy much liked women in general. His attitude wasn't all about keeping them from wearing the badge. That said…he's the victim, not a suspect."

"We do need to find out whether he's antagonized anyone lately."

"That may be hard, given how many people the average patrol officer interacts with every day, even not counting his free time." Matson sighed. "We should talk to his ex-wife first. Friends. All the usual, even if we suspect his death is really the opening move from Dorrance."

Melinda visibly swallowed. "He played such a small part. If this *was* Dorrance, we need to widen our net, make sure we've warned even the bit players."

"Everyone on the prosecutorial *and* defense sides," Daniel agreed. "Paralegals, legal secretaries. What about jail guards? How long did we hold him before he was moved to Salem?"

They threw around more ideas. Boyd offered to help make calls, and Daniel promised to email him a list with numbers. Lieutenant Matson was going to assign another detective, however shorthanded that made them, to look into this murder as potentially having a personal angle. Melinda shook her head when Boyd asked if she'd yet spoken to the two women rescued from Dorrance's house.

"They've done a good job of disappearing. I'm still working at finding them."

Understandably, given that it had been only a few hours since they'd learned about Dorrance's release.

"I didn't see Jonas's phone," Boyd commented.

"Unless it's under his body, it's not there," Daniel said flatly.

"What about a laptop? Doesn't look like he had a desktop."

"I have a call into the station," Melinda said. "He could have left it there. I don't see him using it a lot at home."

Boyd gritted his teeth. "He'd have contacts on it."

"Probably more on his phone, but...yeah." That hesitation revealed some unease. He wasn't telling her anything that hadn't already crossed her mind.

"Friends and some of his coworkers might know if he kept both devices password protected," Matson said briskly. "Let's find out. Daniel, you stay to supervise the scene. Melinda can go back to searching for people we haven't reached. Boyd, if you can help with contacts once she's found phone numbers, that would be a help. I'd like to think none of this will impact your department, but I'm not betting on it. Some of these people have to live outside the city limits."

That was safe to say.

"All right." Boyd rolled his shoulders. "I'll get out of here. I'll be close at hand at sheriff's department headquarters if anything breaks."

The building, and his official office, was right on the outskirts of Sadler, centrally located in this sprawling county with ranches, smaller towns and miles of high mountain desert.

"Let's plan a meeting at nine tomorrow morning," Matson added. "I'd be glad to have you join us, Sheriff."

"Of course," he agreed.

Resisting the temptation to ask Melinda to walk him out, he set out across the brown lawn, his military-honed sense of caution having him placing a hand on the butt of his gun in preparation for rounding the corner of the house.

He hadn't taken more than a few strides when a faint buzz reached him. Text or notification on someone's phone, but not his. Boyd didn't even know why he stopped to look back. They'd all be busy on their phones today.

But he saw that it was Melinda who held her phone in her hand, her expression shocked.

He wheeled and went back. "What is it?"

Her gaze lifted from the phone until her green-gold eyes met his. "It's *him*."

"Dorrance?"

Her head bobbed. She held out the phone so he could read the text.

One down. Now you know I keep promises. All of them.

What was it Dorrance had said in court? *I'll pay you back. Every last one of you.*

"Why the hell would he take the chance of communicating with you?" Daniel asked.

"Because it's all about her." Boyd had to look away from her face. He'd just wandered into a nightmare. A woman he…not loved, but could have loved, had a bull's-eye painted on her back. And he didn't even have to ask if she'd be smart enough to take herself out of this killer's game and let other people hunt down Gene Dorrance like the rabid dog he was. No, Melinda was constitutionally unable to admit to any vulnerability.

She wouldn't like knowing that protecting *her* had just become his priority number one.

Chapter Four

Once Melinda took one of the two remaining seats at the table in the conference room the next morning, she looked around. Only one chair was still empty, the one at the head of the table, left conspicuously open by Lieutenant Matson. As primary on this investigation, Daniel walked in on her heels and took that spot.

Melinda hadn't been able to help noticing Boyd as soon as she stepped through the doorway. His presence was enough to make her nerve endings prickle. Big and handsome, with dark hair grown out from the almost-military haircut she remembered, he had a dominant air that would be easy to resent.

Forcing herself to look away from him, she saw that he'd brought along Miguel Cordova, now a detective with the sheriff's department and, unfortunately, possibly on Dorrance's list of targets. Two additions were a younger SPD detective Melinda had worked with a few times, Emmett Yates and Tom Alvarez, the only uniformed officer at the table.

Everyone present had either a laptop or a notebook

in front of them, and most had grabbed a cup of coffee on the way in. Boyd's, she saw out of the corner of her eye, was a tall hot drink of some kind from a drive-through coffee kiosk she often frequented herself.

The hand holding the cup was large, darkly tanned and, she had reason to know, calloused.

Damn it.

Daniel rapped lightly on the tabletop. "I'll get us started. I've spoken to Dr. Neale, who has already completed the autopsy on Jonas."

Nobody winced, but Melinda felt sure she wasn't the only one who didn't want to picture a man she'd worked with for years naked and cut open.

"She didn't offer any surprises. As we speculated, the cause of death was the deep slice across his throat. Serrated blade, she says, probably a commonly found hunting knife that could have been purchased just about anywhere. I've asked one of our crime analysts to check on local sources, although Dorrance likely purchased the knife before he got to Sadler."

"Do we know yet who else was in contacts in Jonas's phone and/or his laptop?" Boyd asked.

Didn't it figure he'd zero in on that. She'd seen how disturbed he'd been by that text, probably because it came to her. Although why he'd care now, she didn't know.

"No." Daniel sounded grim. "At this point, we need to assume the worst for those law enforcement personnel involved however tangentially in Dorrance's arrest. On the positive side, although Jonas may well have had me and Officer Alvarez listed in his phone, neither of us was involved in bringing down Dorrance. Also positive, I can't think of any reason Jonas would have had any contact info for the two original victims or anyone on the prosecutorial or defense teams. Still, they don't have as much reason to protect their names and addresses as law enforcement officers do. That also leaves the lieutenant and other members of our department unless they've had reason to change their numbers. Lieutenant?"

"Nothing has changed," he said tersely.

"Detective Cordova, what about you?"

Miguel Cordova was in his midthirties, Melinda guessed, not than five foot eight or nine, with a stocky build and a likable face. He shook his head now. "I've had the same number since I took the job with SPD twelve years ago. I did move when I got married two years ago."

Although everyone here probably knew her answers, Melinda volunteered the information that, like Miguel, she'd retained the same phone number but also had moved.

Daniel nodded. "Good. My next point should be obvious to everyone, but I'll say it anyway. You need to be hyperalert from now on. Make sure you're not being followed when you go home."

Cordova looked alarmed, but that worry had already occurred to Melinda and probably the rest of them. It would be heightened for those who had spouses and kids at home.

"First steps," Daniel continued. "I'm sending Emmett to Salem to learn anything he can about Dorrance. The warden sounds like he'll be cooperative. They're searching their records right now to determine whether he had any visitors, for example. Counseling sessions remain confidential, but they'll allow Emmett to interview Dorrance's former cellmates. We need to know whether Dorrance had or has any friends inside the walls or outside."

"Did he have a ride waiting when he walked out?" Melinda asked.

Daniel shook his head. "Taxi. I have a call into the company to find out where he was dropped in hopes we can start tracing him from that end."

"I don't see him taking the Greyhound bus from Salem," she said. "So what's he driving? Where did he get it?"

"That's an excellent question. Lieutenant, any chance we can get a warrant for Dorrance's bank accounts? Assuming he had a penny left after paying his attorneys, he's likely to have pulled out cash. That wouldn't help us track him down, but people do dumb things."

Yes, they did. Half the crooks arrested got caught because they'd made jaw-droppingly stupid mistakes.

"If Sheriff Chaney is making you available, Detective Cordova," Daniel continued, "trying to find out what Dorrance is driving might be something you could take on. Assuming he picked up wheels right away, did he visit a used-car lot? Check out ads online? Rent one initially? We need a vehicle make and model and, better yet, license plate number."

The detective glanced at Boyd, who nodded but said, "Dorrance presumably owned a car before his arrest. Are we sure he doesn't still own the same one?"

"Another good question—" Daniel made a note "—although would he want to drive it? His license has expired, of course, and he hasn't renewed it. His tabs would have, too. Still, if his car was nondescript enough and he stole a set of plates, that might pass unnoticed."

Melinda raised the other obvious question. "If he kept his car, where has it been all these years? If nobody was starting it regularly for him, would it even run?"

"Unlikely," Daniel agreed.

Boyd acknowledged her point with the slightest tip of his head, but shifted directions. "I don't like the fact that he directly contacted Detective McIntosh to taunt her. What if she were to change her number?"

Matson frowned. "That would likely enrage him."

"Should we be pandering to his crap?" Boyd leaned forward. "If he's cut off, that might shake him up a little."

"We can learn something from his communications." Melinda didn't let herself so much as glance at Boyd. Didn't it figure he was worried about the only woman at the table? "Any glimpse into his head is better than a vacuum."

Boyd opened his mouth again, but Daniel said,

"I agree. I also think that you should consider staying with one of us since it's possible Dorrance has your address."

"How could he?" she argued. "Why would Guy have known or cared where I live?"

"He probably didn't, but it's not hard these days to pluck addresses off the internet. You know you'd be welcome to stay with Lindsay and me." His eyes, darker than the golden-brown of Boyd's, met hers.

She smiled crookedly. "Thank you, but for now I'd rather not be scared out of my own home."

Had that rough sound—a growl?—come from Boyd? Probably, although she knew darn well that most men like the ones sitting around this table were programmed to see any woman as more vulnerable than themselves.

Daniel's eyebrows rose momentarily, but he didn't let himself react otherwise. "Let's shelve that for the moment. Who have we been able to talk to, and who do we still need to reach?"

IF BOYD THOUGHT for a minute that that bullheaded woman would listen to reason were he to corner her privately, he'd find a way to take her aside after the meeting. As it was, he knew better. What he'd really like was for her to go into hiding, something they were encouraging other potential victims to consider doing. So far, none of the cops on Dorrance's kill list had agreed to do that. They were armed and dangerous, too damned sure they could defend themselves. Yeah, just like Guy Jonas had done, and him a man with twenty-plus years of experience in law enforcement.

No, he hadn't had the advantage of a warning, but how much help would that really be? If he'd had the fan running in the bathroom, it would have drowned out the sound of an intrusion. People relaxed when they were home.

Did any of them have a security system? Had any of them so much as pulled their gun on the job, never mind fired it? Practice at the gun range was fine, but given only a split second to respond, using deadly force didn't come naturally for people, even cops. He'd be more willing to bet on someone who'd done combat duty in the military, but even for seasoned soldiers, reaction times would gradually slow depending on how long it had been since the individual rejoined the civilian world. Boyd was well aware that even keeping his skills sharp the way he tried to do was no guarantee.

Shutting down his wandering thoughts, Boyd made himself focus on the meeting. He'd made a bunch of the calls himself yesterday afternoon and evening and had been able to reach almost everyone. An assistant prosecutor had taken another job and left the area several years ago. Boyd was still looking for her. The sitting judge for the trial had retired to Florida.

"He does have a security system on his home," Boyd reported now. "Says he can't imagine anyone going that far to hunt him down, but he sleeps better having it. He'll take precautions from now on, until we let him know we've nailed Dorrance."

"Good." Daniel shifted his gaze. "Melinda?"

"I spoke to Andrea Kudelka's mother. She and her husband relocated to Idaho." She grimaced. "They wanted to be near family."

"Just to make them easy to trace," Matson muttered.

"You'd think that would have occurred to them." When she shook her head, light shimmered on her sleek dark hair, pulled into her usual knot at her nape. "However, the mom told me that Andrea is living under another name—and no, she didn't go to court to get it changed—and isn't near her parents. The mother said it's really hard not being able to see her, but even with Dorrance in prison, Andrea didn't feel safe. Also, she was being stalked by reporters who wanted follow-up interviews. She said she wasn't about to end up on the cover of some tabloid at the checkout stand."

Good for her, Boyd thought.

"The mother will pass on the bad news and our warning. I feel more comfortable knowing she's not in the area."

There were nods all around.

"I also located Erica Warner's father—apparently her parents are now divorced—and he listened to me for about two minutes, said, 'If you'd done your damn job searching for her when she disappeared originally, she wouldn't have suffered the way she did,' and hung up on me."

There was a moment of shared silence. Every failure was a weight that burdened any cop with a conscience. As well as she hid her emotions, Boyd didn't like seeing the expression on Melinda's face.

Lieutenant Matson must have seen it, too, because he said sharply, "You're the last person he should dump on. It's only thanks to you we found Erica and Andrea at all or followed up as hard as we did to try to determine if he'd had other victims."

She lifted one shoulder. "Not like that paid off."

Matson opened his mouth, but she shook her head and he subsided.

Daniel had been watching the exchange, but now he said, "Detectives Yates and Cordova have their assignments. For the rest of us, I think we can agree that finding this scumbag is our first priority. At least we know who we're looking for. We need to identify places that would have been available to rent a few days ago, vacant buildings where he could squat, anyone camping outside designated private and public parks. Sergeant Alvarez, I'm asking you to get the word to patrol officers to keep a sharp eye out for anyplace that appears to be newly inhabited. Sheriff, I assume you'll do the same county-wide."

"I will," Boyd agreed, "but we all know how expansive this county is. It's like trying to pick out one sagebrush from another."

They agreed that bringing in volunteers wasn't an option. The county did own a helicopter, which Boyd would get up in the air doing a search pattern immediately—and keep it in the air to the extent his budget allowed.

And beyond, he vowed silently. He could afford to foot the bill for a few days. The faster they found Gene Dorrance, the sooner Boyd could let go of this painful cramping beneath his breastbone.

They decided to go ahead with a press conference, too, which would be conducted by the police chief once Matson briefed him. The lieutenant had been the lead detective investigating Dorrance, which meant keeping him out of the public eye—unless, at some point, they decided to wave the red cape to draw Dorrance's attention.

Daniel glanced around, said, "Unless anyone has something else to say, let's get busy. We can reconvene tomorrow morning, same time."

Chairs scraped back. Most people were on their feet when Boyd said, "No reason to hold most of you up, but I have some questions for Lieutenant Matson and Detective McIntosh. Just background."

Daniel eyed him and sat back down, as he had the right to do. The younger detectives and Alvarez hustled out. Melinda narrowed her eyes but didn't protest.

Once the door had shut behind the others, the lieutenant spoke up. "What is it?"

"I want to know why Dorrance is focused on Detective McIntosh." He paused, let his voice drop to a near growl. "Most of all, I need to understand why any judge okayed the warrant to search his house."

MELINDA'S HANDS TIGHTENED, the one under the table into a tight fist. Her nails bit into her palm. Since she still held her laptop, she hoped no one else noticed her whitened knuckles on that hand.

She worked really hard to wipe her face clean of expression before looking at him. "Are you implying that the warrant was improper?"

His gaze drilled her. "Unless my copy of the file is abridged, I'm saying the evidence presented to the judge seems thin."

Almost all of that evidence had come from her observations since Guy Jonas had disputed some of it and disagreed with her conclusions.

This was a direct challenge by Boyd, and, yeah, she was taking it personally. He had—what?—a whole year and a half of law enforcement experience, and he thought he knew better than she did?

Before she could fire back, Daniel said mildly, "I admit I wondered about the same thing. I'm not criticizing—if the investigation had stalled, I'm guessing Dorrance would have seized the chance to kill the two women and dispose of their bodies. That we were able to go in fast saved those women's lives. But I'll admit it seems as if the judge ruled in your favor based on some…impressions, rather than hard evidence." The pause was almost delicate.

Melinda suspected that Daniel wouldn't have raised this subject, or would have done so with her alone, but it worried her that he'd stumbled over the same thing Boyd had. Although why should it? The warrant was granted. They'd found the two women imprisoned in the basement of Gene Dorrance's house, Andrea in particularly bad shape after taking a recent, severe beating, and the jury hadn't hesitated to convict Dorrance.

I was right.

"What difference does it make now?" she asked, knowing she sounded frosty but not caring.

"It probably doesn't," Boyd said slowly, "although I wonder how a guy convicted of a crime this ugly ended up being recommended for the pardon." He raised his eyebrows at Matson. "Is there any way to find out?"

Feeling under attack, Melinda snapped, "Again, what difference does it make? We know he's here. We know he murdered a Sadler PD officer."

"I like to be sure my footing is solid," he shot back. "You sound defensive. That makes me nervous."

She was. Melinda tried for some deep breathing without letting it be obvious that's what she was doing. She tried to read the lieutenant's expression. Had he doubted her then? He was being awfully quiet now.

"Let's start with the 911 call," Boyd continued inexorably. "The woman heard a scream. A long, continuing one that was abruptly cut off."

Daniel looked inquiring, so she said, "That's right. By the way, I don't think I said, but I tracked her down yesterday. She and her husband moved away shortly after the arrest. She said she couldn't stand knowing what had been going on next door all that time. They're in Arizona now."

Daniel and Matson nodded. Boyd's gaze stayed steady.

You're stalling.

"By chance, Guy and I were only a couple of blocks away. We got there really fast, talked to her before knocking on Dorrance's door. She was certain the scream had come from his house. It sounded terrified, not like teenagers playing around. She was sure it had been a woman, but the sound was muted as if by walls. She might not have heard it at all, but the houses are on average size city lots, and hers didn't have a garage, only a carport and maybe twenty feet of grass separating her kitchen from his house." She took a deep breath. "So then we rang his doorbell."

"Had you used lights or sirens?" Boyd asked.

"No. Dorrance looked both flustered and mad when he threw the door open. He also appeared… disheveled. He was breathing hard, and his shirt was missing a couple of buttons. It was half tucked in, half yanked out. I was sure I saw a deep scratch on his neck."

"I seem to remember that Jonas didn't see it," Matson commented.

Oh, *now* he had something to say, but Melinda was sure Boyd already knew that Jonas thought she was imagining things. In fact, he had claimed not to notice anything off about the guy who'd come to the door. Dorrance was home after a day at work. What did she expect, he'd be wearing a crisp white shirt and tie? During the one year she'd been stuck working with Guy, she'd especially hated partnering with him on domestic violence calls. He gave off a definite vibe that he thought a man's home was his castle, that cops had no business butting in. He'd never said it, but she assumed that in his worldview the king of the castle had the right to backhand his woman if he felt like it.

Okay, maybe that wasn't true, but his attitude had rubbed her wrong.

Deciding not to address any of that, she said calmly, "No, but he didn't have the same angle I did. He stood to one side and toward the back of the porch." The defensive position when there were two of them was standard practice. "I asked to speak to anyone else who was home."

Even all these years later, she remembered that moment vividly. Her every instinct had prickled. Dorrance had triggered all of her alarms. He'd been sweating, giving off waves of anger and violence. She'd have said he looked crazy, although she'd had experience by then with mentally ill people acting strangely, and never felt the deep-down certainty that there was something seriously *wrong* in that house.

The three men watching her waited.

Melinda stared back at them, feeling suddenly as if she was on trial—and Sheriff Boyd Chaney was the judge and maybe jury, too. Was he jumping on this now in hopes of getting her fired from the investigation?

Chapter Five

Not so much resentful as anxious, Melinda didn't see any way out of answering Boyd's questions. Both Daniel and the lieutenant outranked her.

The really uncomfortable part was the sense that she'd been thrown into a flashback. Shifting in her seat, she said, "He insisted he lived alone. There wasn't anyone else there. He was obviously furious to have to defend himself. That flake who'd called 911 must have heard the television, but when I asked what he'd been watching, he got flustered. He retreated to say, 'I didn't mean my TV. It could have been anyone's on the block.'"

She knew what they were thinking. On any other call like that, she and Jonas would have politely retreated, fearing they'd been played, not liking it, but not suspecting anything worse than an argument that had gotten out of hand.

"I guess it was just a gut feeling," she said finally. "I tried to see as much as I could past him. There were dirty dishes on a TV tray pushed away from a recliner in the living room, yet in the hall behind him, some food sat on a cookie sheet obviously being used as a tray that I suspected he'd set down when the doorbell rang."

I suspected. Yep, she'd gone out on a limb there.

"Two sandwiches on paper plates, two plastic bottles of water. Right next to the small table, a door was a few inches ajar. I felt…a draft of cold air coming from the house."

"He could have had the air-conditioning running," Boyd said.

"He could have, but I didn't hear it." She tipped up her chin and met his implacable gaze. "I also got a whiff of something really bad, like a sewer spill, and I saw a streak of what I was sure was blood on the door molding. And then—" she swallowed "—I heard a woman crying out, or sobbing. *Really* muffled, but under the circumstances…"

"So you apologized for your intrusion, left and reported what you'd seen and heard to…"

"Me," the lieutenant said. "My then partner, who retired not that much later, and I did some research on Dorrance. You know that." He nodded at the closed laptop in front of Boyd.

"Sure. He'd been accused of rape when he lived in northern California, but was never charged."

"The investigator there told me there'd been whispers about this guy for a while. The accuser wasn't the first, but she was the most credible. Unfortunately, she'd let a few days go by after the alleged attack, showered and bathed repeatedly, so there was no physical evidence, and no witnesses. Dorrance claimed he hardly knew the woman, but said they'd had a run-in after a fender bender, which was true. When I asked questions here in Sadler, I found women universally steered clear of him. He came on to them aggressively. People were uneasy because it was obvious he liked younger women. A lot younger. Even his employer, who rated him as a competent mechanic, didn't like the guy. Felt uncomfortable around him."

Boyd leaned back in his chair. Melinda kept her gaze fixed on the pattern of the teal-and-purple-paisley sleeve holding her laptop. Matson…she couldn't tell without studying him closely.

"So you got a warrant to search the house based on a guy whose background was sketchy, but who had never so much as been arrested, and Detective McIntosh's testimony that she thought she'd seen a smear of blood—"

She lifted her head to glare at him. "I did see it!"

"That Dorrance looked as if he'd been in a tussle, that he'd made two sandwiches that he might or might not have been taking down to the basement, and that something was up with the plumbing."

"And that when we went back to talk to the neighbor, she said she was bothered by the smell almost every time she went out in her backyard. She knew Dorrance was out in his yard daily, rinsing something out."

"Uh-huh." Boyd lifted his arms, stretching. Well-honed muscles in his chest and shoulders flexed. "There'd have been a *real* stink if the cops went in and found nothing but maybe a plumbing issue down in the basement."

"We knew we were taking a risk," Matson admitted. "We also knew we'd had at least four young women—teenagers—go missing in the past few years. One witness had seen a man who met Dorrance's appearance snatch Andrea Kudelka. What she saw then didn't get investigators anywhere, but when we tied it to Melinda's description along with her suspicions…" He trailed off.

Boyd lifted one eyebrow. "What you really mean is, to Melinda's gut feeling."

Nobody said a word.

After a moment that hummed with tension, Boyd nodded. "As it happens, I have a lot of respect for gut feelings. My own and teammates' saved our lives a few times. Thanks for answering my questions."

He collected his things, pushed back his chair and left after tossing the empty coffee cup in the metal trash container. A moment later, Matson stood too, paused to squeeze Melinda's shoulder, then walked out with Daniel.

Melinda sat unmoving, feeling as if she'd just been upended and shaken. Why had Boyd started that, and once he had, why hadn't he expressed doubt in her competence?

And, God help her, how had he known which part she'd lied about?

MELINDA HAD ONLY been a cop for a few years when the judge granted that warrant based on her testimony, Boyd reflected. That said something important about her. She had to have already earned a high level of respect from the local judiciary as well as her fellow cops.

Except from Guy Jonas, Boyd suspected, reading between the lines. Clearly, Dorrance had had no idea that Jonas would have shrugged and walked away after that first door-knock if it had been left to him.

What intrigued Boyd was his suspicion that Melinda had lied in the report used to get the warrant. He would have guessed her to be a by-the-book cop. *Being* a cop meant too much to her for her to risk her job, but he had no doubt she'd done so.

That said, he and she had worked together on a serial killer investigation, and a few times she'd demonstrated something he could best call intuition. He'd actually been spooked by it once or twice. At the time, he'd told himself again that getting involved with her had been a mistake from the beginning. Boyd didn't want anyone able to see too deeply inside him. His ranger teammates—men like Gabe Decker and Leon Cabrera—had their own nightmares. It wasn't anything they had to talk about. Sooner or later, Melinda would have expected him to answer the questions he'd seen in her eyes.

Frowning as he walked into the ugly, single-story building that housed the sheriff's department, Boyd thought, *So find yourself a pretty, shallow woman who likes sex and would enjoy living on a thriving ranch*. Too bad he couldn't work up a lot of enthusiasm. Seeing Melinda again, and two days in a row at that, had revved up his libido, but the focus seemed to be 100 percent on her.

Damn it, they had to catch this scumbag, and fast.

Consigning his budget to hell, he made a plan with the pilot of the helicopter that would keep him in the air as long as the light lasted and sent him on his way. Fortunately, the deputy had seemed to get what Boyd was telling him, however vague it was, but until they had a make, model and color of a vehicle to watch for, there wasn't a lot to pinpoint. Places that look like they might have a squatter or a new renter or homeowner. Single man—Boyd had armed the pilot with what photos they had of Dorrance, although they hadn't yet received an updated one from the prison. Maybe someone who saw the helicopter flying low and dashed for cover.

Boyd grimaced at his memory of a time when drug traffickers here in the county had employed an unarmed helicopter in their search for a little girl in hiding because she'd witnessed the massacre of her family. Boyd and probably half the other ranchers had thrown a fit because their animals hadn't liked the low-flying aircraft.

This time, people would understand—but he'd just as soon mention of the helicopter didn't appear in any news story.

If only Dorrance was dumb enough to never look up.

By the next morning meeting, all Boyd could think was, *A watched pot doesn't boil*. Or should it be, *Not a creature was stirring*? Well, except for the reporters massed outside. Usually a big story meant half a dozen reporters and cameramen showed up, but today's crowd was double that, and this wasn't for a press conference. When he drove past, someone spotted him, and several ran down the sidewalk shouting questions he couldn't hear with his window rolled up. He'd been grateful to be able to pull into the parking lot behind the station, protected today by a uniformed cop.

The somewhat smaller group—lacking both Emmett Yates and Tom Alvarez—gathered around the table in the conference room at the police station, Boyd seeing that he wasn't the only one feeling increased tension.

Daniel began, tone wry. "Yesterday's press conference was a success, as you'll have noticed. We may be sorry, and I'm not talking about the fact that we may have trouble heading out without an entourage. The phones are ringing off the hook."

Boyd nodded. "Sheriff's department, too." He had a bad feeling he'd be spending a good part of his day answering the calls and evaluating tips. So far, he didn't have much of a role otherwise.

"Nothing useful to this point," Daniel added, "although most of our officers are now occupied following up on the information." Muscles bulged in his jaws. "The problem is made worse after we ordered that no one check out a possible hideout without a partner. If this goes on long, I'm thinking we need to talk about bringing in help."

Boyd nodded his agreement. He had no idea how

much help—the boots on the ground kind—the FBI would bring in, versus them sending an agent or two to advise. Or whether the FBI would be impressed by a manhunt spurred by a long-ago threat and one dead cop.

Plus the text claiming credit, of course.

"Emmett expects to be back late this afternoon," Daniel continued. "I'd have had him join us on his phone, except that so far all he's learned is that the guy had no friends. Not a single visitor. He wasn't real popular with his cellmates, either."

That wasn't unexpected, Boyd reflected. Pedophiles were probably the most despised among any prison population—well, except for cops—but someone like Dorrance who had imprisoned and brutalized two very young women over the course of years was unlikely to stir warm feelings in men who, while they'd committed crimes, quite often violent ones, nonetheless had wives or girlfriends and daughters. There was that indefinable quality, too, the one that made anyone in close quarters with Gene Dorrance "uncomfortable."

"Detective Cordova?" Daniel prompted. "Do you have anything for us?"

"Nothing very helpful yet."

Having encountered Cordova in the hall, Boyd had heard this report from his detective just before they walked into the conference room.

"Dorrance must have stashed some money at some point, or someone owed him, because he did buy a car immediately—the taxi delivered him to a home where he was able to pay cash for an old Toyota pickup on its last legs. Bright yellow," he added. "He may not have known the color and how conspicuous it would be until he set eyes on it. It was found abandoned in a mall parking lot hours later."

Matson leaned forward. "Was a car stolen from the lot…?"

Cordova shook his head. "None have been reported stolen as of now. It's not impossible—apparently the outskirt of the lot is often used as an informal park-and-ride, and possibly a place to leave cars for people who are going to be away for a few days. It's a constant hassle for mall security, I was told. It seems more likely, though, that Dorrance met someone else who was selling a vehicle privately. What if he spotted one with a 'for sale' sign in the window, for example, and arranged to meet at the mall?"

"In other words, a car that wasn't even posted on Craigslist or the like," the lieutenant said flatly.

"Right. Used-car lots had a few sales in the day and a half we're focused on, but nobody recalled seeing anyone meeting Dorrance's description. Also, that kind of sales force typically insists on seeing a driver's license and proof of insurance before allowing anyone to take a car off the lot."

"We need to get his face on the news in Salem, too," Melinda said, voice tight.

Daniel nodded. "We're already on that. I know KOIN Channel 6 and KPTV Fox 12 covered the story. We may get lucky."

There were nods all around.

"Boyd, anything?"

"The county commissioners aren't happy. Their phones are ringing off the hook, too. I assume your mayor isn't enjoying the turmoil, either."

The lieutenant was the one to answer dryly. "That's one way to put it. Chief Austin isn't thrilled either, given that we've conscripted most of the police force. Let's pray we have a brief break in typical crime."

"I've been checking in daily with all potential victims that I made initial contact with," Boyd said. "I assume you're doing the same?"

Everyone nodded.

Boyd already knew that Dorrance had been released back then on bail to await trial. He could have used the time to stalk police officers and anyone else he blamed for his predicament. Maybe he didn't act out his revenge then because he still hoped he might not be convicted. Could be his hopes had had something to do with the warrant.

Still, that he'd killed so quickly after returning to town suggested he hadn't had to do the expected research; he already knew where Jonas lived.

Melinda had been uncharacteristically quiet thus far.

Studying her, Boyd said, "Melinda, Dorrance was arrested in the first place because of your gut feeling. So what's your gut telling you now?" He didn't like her involvement, but as long as she was being stubborn, they'd all be fools not to take advantage of her instincts. "Will he want to drag this out, enjoy watching us chase our tails? He had to have made his first kill practically the minute he hit town. Is he stalking a second victim? Looking for an easy opportunity?"

Her face appeared pinched, plainer than usual. "I do think taunting is part of his satisfaction. He needed to get our attention, so he killed Guy right away. Now? What's the hurry?" She took and released a deep breath. "This is a man who in essence engaged in long-term torture with his kidnap victims. Watching them suffer, deteriorate physically, lose hope, all had to be a big part of what gave him a charge. That… might be applicable to his campaign to pay us back."

Daniel's forehead creased. "That makes sense."

"Does he already have a place to stay? Might he have had an idea even before he got to Sadler?"

"That's possible. Any long-time resident in the area notices vacant houses and thinks things like, 'One of these years, that roof is going to fall in if no one replaces it.'"

"If he hadn't showed up in Sadler so soon, I might have suspected that he'd found a way to buy fake ID," Matson commented. "That would have allowed him to potentially rent, say from an out-of-town landlord who wouldn't hear what's going on right now. As it is…" He shrugged.

Afraid something else was going on in Melinda's head, Boyd kept watching her. Despite her efforts to look anywhere but at him, she must have been aware of his scrutiny, because she turned her head suddenly.

Her eyes fully met his, and he flinched at what he was afraid might be anguish. "I…had a thought during the night. We stole something from him seven years ago. It's the something that made him feel strong, in control and gratified him."

Oh, hell. All Boyd could think was that he should have thought of that. Now they had to pile on another worry: that a young woman was about to snatched— or already had been.

"YES, MA'AM," MELINDA said into her phone. "You have a new neighbor who makes you nervous." She held her pen poised above the notepad. "Can you tell me when he moved in?"

"Well, the apartment has been rented for almost a month, but I didn't see the new resident until recently. I mean, someone was going in and out and turning the music up too loud—I've complained twice to the manager, and she hasn't done a darn thing as far as I can tell!—but this man you're looking for could have had someone else rent him a place, couldn't he? And he has been quiet this week. I just don't like the way he looks at me."

He also could have murdered a resident and taken over the lease, so to speak.

The day pretty much stunk, as they all had since that idiot governor had blithely released a man set on vengeance. Melinda had spent the day taking an endless stream of calls and wasn't at all surprised that most were so far off, they didn't even justify follow-up. Despite her passing thought, this one sounded awfully unlikely—she couldn't imagine Dorrance would choose to take over an apartment with multiple near-neighbors and poor soundproofing. There certainly was no indication he had anyone at all who'd have rented a place in advance for him. And when had Dorrance learned he was going to be released anyway? she wondered. She hadn't thought to ask.

Still, it was always worth paying attention when a woman mentioned a single guy who made her uneasy. The vague physical description of a man who could be Dorrance would have kept Melinda listening to this particular caller anyway.

"When did you see this man for the first time?" she asked.

The slight hesitation gave her a clue.

"Well, it was probably ten days ago, but I wasn't sure you knew exactly when the man you're looking for might have gotten out of prison. I mean, maybe they just don't want to admit they let him go sooner than they were supposed to."

Instead of banging her head on her desk, Melinda wrote down the woman's name, phone number and address before picking up the next call.

Daniel was doing the same not far from her, as was Emmett Yates, returned from his jaunt to Salem, along with one other detective, Lieutenant Matson and several patrol officers. Every so often Daniel would glance at her and shake his head or roll his eyes. At the moment, Emmett seemed to be trying to wrench his hair out while listening on his phone. She totally understood the impulse.

Having stayed late, Melinda finally left the station

to find the sun heading down, but daylight still hold-ing. Sunset wasn't until almost nine o'clock in early July. Parking should be secure here surrounded by high chain-link fencing behind the brick-built police station, but she still kept an eye out on the way to her Subaru. Thank goodness, the press corps seemed to have given up for the day. She still kept an eye out, but nobody followed her from the station across town to the gro-cery store that was closest to her house, a Thriftway. There, she scanned the parking lot, not seeing any-one just sitting in a vehicle. An aisle away, a woman was lifting a toddler out of the back seat of a minivan.

Nobody in the store looked familiar either, not even the clerks. She didn't usually shop this late.

Normally, Melinda came with a list, having planned meals she actually intended to cook from scratch, but today she just tossed whatever caught her eye into her cart. She bought lots of salad mak-ings and a few frozen, microwaveable meals, went through the self-check station and loaded her bags in the back of her Subaru. She clicked the key fob to unlock her vehicle and slid in behind the wheel be-fore she saw something that hadn't been here when she went into the store.

A white, business-sized envelope, fatter than it should be if it held only a folded sheet or two of paper, lay askew on the seat.

And on the front of the envelope, her name was printed in slashing strokes that were oddly childlike.

Her hand closed convulsively on the butt of her Glock.

Chapter Six

Knowing that he was being damned unreasonable didn't keep Boyd from being furious that Melinda hadn't called him. It was Daniel who had, and by now there'd already been a fruitless canvass of shoppers coming and going at the grocery store in hopes of finding a witness who'd seen someone gaining access to her car.

Glad that when his phone rang he hadn't made it all the way home, Boyd did a U-turn in the middle of the highway and drove straight to the police station, where the envelope was to be opened by a crime scene investigator to be sure no evidence was lost by doing it carelessly.

Striding into the basement room where the limited CSI facilities were consigned, Boyd nodded at the woman he already knew. She'd likely been called in from home, too. Otherwise, Daniel, Melinda and Matson stood around a tall table. At least they hadn't opened the damn envelope yet, he saw, even though he didn't know why it mattered that they'd waited for him.

Melinda looked stoic, but she had to be feeling unsettled.

"Any idea how this creep got into Detective McIntosh's car?" he asked brusquely.

"We've fingerprinted just in case," Daniel said, "but we suspect he used a screwdriver or the like to crack open the passenger-side window. You know how quickly that can be done."

Boyd did. Cops carried a tool designed to do exactly that for citizens who'd locked their keys inside. They got plenty of practice utilizing that tool. He already knew that Melinda had been driving her Forester for ten years or so, meaning it predated some of the fancier security protections.

"We think that's what Dorrance did when he abducted Erica Warner." Melinda sounded strained, if Boyd was any judge. "We had a witness who caught sight of what was happening. He was apparently crouched behind the driver's seat of Erica's car when she got in after work. Coworkers and family said she always locked her car."

It wouldn't take more than a minute to crack the window, unlock the door, slip in and relock before crawling into the back. That's why motorists in general and women in particular were urged to scan the interior of their cars *before* they unlocked and climbed in. Melinda had presumably done that tonight, but she'd been looking for a person, not a message.

Boyd's mouth tightened.

He nodded at the envelope, lying on a sheet of

heavy white paper torn off a big roll. "Let's see what we have."

The tech carefully slit the top of the envelope, commented, "It's self-stick," then cracked it open with her latex-covered fingers. "Hair," she said after a minute. I think that's all that's in there."

Boyd couldn't be the only one who stiffened.

She picked up the envelope and tilted it so that everyone could see what, indeed, appeared to be a coil of brown hair. Then she tipped it out onto the white paper.

They all gaped. It wasn't a full head of hair, but it was long enough—ten or twelve inches—to suggest the likelihood that it was a woman's hair. That wouldn't necessarily be so in more liberal western Washington, but in these parts, not many men wore theirs long enough that it could be captured in a ponytail.

"Snipped off, or shaved from a head?" Daniel asked.

Either way, the cut was clean.

"We need to check again on every woman on our list," Matson said. "And what about Kudelka and Warner?"

Melinda shook her head. "Unless this is dyed. Andrea is a blonde. Erica's hair had a tinge of red. This…" She bent forward so that her nose was almost touching the coil. "Jen, do I see some gray strands?"

The three men leaned forward, too, Boyd squinting to focus. Yeah, he saw the gray, too. This hair didn't come from a young woman.

The tech produced a magnifying glass and examined the sample more closely. "Definitely gray. No sign that the hair has been dyed."

Daniel straightened. "So not a new victim he picked up for entertainment value."

"Unless..." Melinda stepped back from the table with an abruptness that caught all their attention before drawing a deep breath and looking at her fellow cops. "I could be way off, but what if he did have in mind a house that would work for his purposes, only it wasn't vacant?"

Daniel swore. "You think he killed the occupant?"

"Maybe, but what if he knew of an older woman who didn't hold a job? Retired, maybe, a loner? Someone who wouldn't be missed if she wasn't seen regularly."

"He likes them young. Would he be interested in raping this woman?"

"What he really likes is to make women suffer." Melinda didn't sound like herself. "That may be his primary need, not actual sexual attraction to the victim. And this time around, he can kill two birds with one stone—imprison a woman, torment her and have a comfortable place to stay where no one will pay any attention to lights coming on at night, the sound of a television, maybe even the garbage can being taken out to the curb weekly."

Boyd ran through the scenario in his head and found it appalling logical. So much for the hours they'd wasted looking for the long-vacant house that showed signs of activity that shouldn't be there.

"He'd have access to this woman's car, too," he said. "Even if we're able to find out what he bought, he can garage it and drive something else."

In her astute way, Melinda suggested, "If she's housebound, she might have had groceries delivered, which would cut down on his risk."

"And let's not forget her credit cards," Daniel said grimly.

"Yet he set out in broad daylight to leave this on your car seat." Boyd looked at her. "Why? Is he trying to give you clues?"

Creases formed on her forehead. "Maybe? Or maybe this is more of an up yours. A way of saying, 'I'm smarter than all of you.' He has to know there's no way we can trace whose head this hair came from. Even if we can get DNA tested in the foreseeable future, what are the odds we'd come up with a match?"

Zero, unless this woman had sent a sample to a genealogical website.

What was wrong with the three of them, able to lay a calm veneer over a conversation about such horrific possibilities? And why was this bothering him so much when he'd seen terrible things as a soldier, not to mention the gruesome corpses left by a serial killer and worked that investigation?

But Boyd knew—*that* killer hadn't been interested in Melinda. This one was.

"He had to have followed you."

"I was watching!" Her throat worked. "I was worrying about a reporter waylaying me. I'd swear no one was behind me."

"Unless he picked you up partway," Daniel said, almost gently. "If he knows where you live…"

Boyd's greatest fear. He ground his teeth, but decided to redirect them to the woman who'd just had the haircut. He nodded toward the hair. "How did Dorrance know this person?"

Melinda looked almost grateful. "Maybe he didn't. Maybe he only knew *of* her."

"How?" Boyd fought against a need to pace. "That's what we need to figure out."

"I agree," she said briskly. "We need to learn as much as we can about his routines before his arrest. Drive the route he'd have taken between work and home. Where did he grocery shop?"

"Or did he vary that, so no one paid attention to what he was buying?" Matson suggested. "Or the quantity he was buying?"

She nodded. "Good thought." She sounded energized by the new avenue of investigation. Of course she refused to give in to fear. "He had guns. Did he practice at a local range?"

"Have a gym?" Daniel asked.

"No, there was a weight room at his house. It's not big, only a two bedroom with a full basement. The second bedroom was well-equipped for his workouts."

"Couldn't let himself be overpowered," Daniel said dryly.

"Yet somehow Andrea did knock him aside and make it up the stairs," Melinda reminded them. "Screaming all the way. She'd reached the top before he caught her, slammed her head on the door-jamb and dragged her back down to her cell."

Matson's throat worked. "Where he beat the crap out of her."

"Andrea is a tall woman. Close to my height, as I recall. He might have enjoyed the challenge of capturing a woman who had confidence in her strength. Reducing her to nothingness would be even more satisfying."

Melinda could have been talking about herself.

There was a moment of silence. For all that they sounded more matter-of-fact than Boyd liked—he felt downright crazed—they had to outthink this SOB. Dwelling on the suffering of his victims, including a new one, wouldn't help them catch him.

As extra motivation went, though, rage worked just fine.

"What's happened to Dorrance's house?" he asked.

"I DROVE BY YESTERDAY," Melinda told him. She tried not to look at him, without being obvious about it. Something in his very stillness made her feel as if the air was charged with static electricity that might shock her if she wasn't careful. "The bank had foreclosed on it," she said with false calm. "I knew that, and I guess I assumed it had sold or been rented or something."

"With that history?" Daniel muttered. "I'd have razed the place."

Melinda had been shocked that it still stood. Did the bank officials really think anybody would buy a place with two prison cells in the basement? Would the listing include them as possible den and hobby rooms? How about the bloodstained concrete floors? She'd driven by a few times the first year, but then let it slip from her radar. After all, she knew where Dorrance was.

Until she didn't.

"I...walked around and looked in windows," she said. "Needless to say, they're seriously grimy. I couldn't get in. It didn't look like anybody had done anything to it." The hank of hair on the table drew her gaze again, a source of primal horror. "This decreases the likelihood that we'll find anything there."

"We need to get in anyway," Boyd snapped. "Unless they changed the locks—and if they did, the new ones are probably crap—what's to stop Dorrance from squatting in the basement? Keep a hostage in one space, sleep in the other himself?"

"That's too obvious," Daniel objected.

"And yet he murdered a cop two days ago, and nobody except Melinda has thought to look at his old house."

With a half-shrug, Daniel conceded the point. "I know the manager of the local bank. I'll call him now and ask for permission for us to get in." He left the room, followed by Boyd and Matson. Melinda paused briefly to talk to the tech.

Somehow, she wasn't at all surprised to find Boyd and her lieutenant waiting for her on the main floor.

"There's something we haven't addressed," Boyd said, in the kind of voice that raised her hackles.

This was a man who'd spent years giving orders, and expected instant obedience. He had to know she wouldn't give him what he wanted, and yet he wasn't softening his approach.

Conscious of Lieutenant Matson's presence, she raised her eyebrows. "And that would be?"

"You, Detective McIntosh. That could have been your hair. He wasn't just saying, 'You can't catch me,' he was threatening *you*."

Yes, when she saw what was in the envelope, she'd had a moment of imagining it was hers, that the men were standing around the table talking about where Dorrance could be holding her.

She couldn't think like that. She wouldn't.

With cool poise, she said, "I'll keep doing my job, the same as you will. Dorrance's communications suggest that he won't be in any hurry to attack me. He's enjoying too much being able to contact me when and where he chooses."

The lieutenant cleared his throat. "I have to agree with Sheriff Chaney, Detective. I worry you're minimizing Dorrance's fixation on you. I think there's nothing he'd like better than to lock you in one of his cells."

Matson had never been anything but supportive since promoting her to the detective squad. This felt like a betrayal.

"What, you want me to go into hiding?"

She became suddenly aware that he'd aged a decade in the past couple of days. Even the white in his hair was more noticeable. He said heavily, "I didn't

say that, but you don't like admitting any vulnerability."

"Do any of us?"

If that was a smile, it wasn't very convincing. "No.
You can't do this job if you dwell too much on the
risks. But Sheriff Chaney is right in this case. You've
said yourself, this scum lives to torture women. He
slit Guy Jonas's throat, which is ugly enough, but
quick. Do you think he'd be that merciful to you if
he got his hands on you?"

She wasn't a fool, but she'd worked hard to become as invulnerable as possible. How could she
back down? Let herself depend too much on other
people? She'd be thrown back to a time when she had
no say in her life at all. She'd sworn she wouldn't let
that happen to her again. Never.

"I'm a cop. I'm armed. Andrea Kudelka overpowered him once, and in doing so saved herself and
Erica. You know how that must eat at him? Right
now, what he needs is a captive who is weak enough
to restore his ego. He's *afraid* of me, and he should
be. That's what all this is about."

Boyd's gaze felt like a red-hot laser, but fortunately Daniel rejoined them before Boyd could vent.

"I have permission. Who wants to go?"

"I've seen the house before," Melinda said quickly.
"I can tell if anything has changed."

"You don't need me." Lieutenant Matson stepped
back. "Keep me informed."

Boyd said, "I'm going." No compromise in his
hard voice.

"I want to see it, too," Daniel agreed.

"I can bring you both back here," Boyd suggested. "One vehicle would draw less attention than three."

He was repelled to think of some reporter with gleaming teeth standing in front of the house of horrors as he or she spoke dramatically to the camera.

"Sounds good." Forced into being the referee between her and Boyd in the past, Daniel gave her a look she recognized, one that said, *Play nice*.

And here she thought she'd done so well.

CREAK.

Daniel froze momentarily on the third step from the top of the stairs leading into the basement. Melinda, hovering just above him, cringed. Had that stair always squeaked? If so, it must have worked like a gunshot on the imprisoned women. Gene's way of saying, *Here I come!*

After that brief check during which his back stiffened, Daniel continued. When Melinda reached that step, she stepped well to the side and avoided the squeak. Or maybe it was just her lesser weight, because when she was halfway down, the creak came again under Boyd's foot.

Melinda had only been down here once, and under vastly different circumstances. The electricity had been on, for starters. They hadn't had to rely on flashlights and what grimy light seeped through tattered shades on the windows. There'd been a crowd, too—armored SWAT team members followed by the two detectives, Melinda entering only once Dorrance was cuffed and the scene secured. She'd been included so that a woman officer was present to reassure the two victims.

Today, the air in the house was thick and musty. The three of them had quickly glanced around the main floor, including the weight room, complete with a dust-coated bench and set of barbells. Starting down to the basement, what she breathed in was oppressive and made her want to gag. Could she still smell the feces and urine as well as blood? Or was it all in her imagination?

She didn't ask either of the men.

The half basement would have been cramped even if it hadn't been carved up to create the two cells and a room that held the furnace and hot water tank. A five-by-ten-foot aisle allowed for wall shelves and access to a door and the few concrete steps outside that led up to the backyard. From the outside, they'd seen that the single basement window had been blocked long ago.

Having a moment longer than Boyd and Melinda to look around, Daniel played his flashlight around and said a vicious word. "They didn't do a damn thing down here!"

Somehow, Boyd had covered his left hand with a latex glove. He cautiously opened the first door, then just stood in the opening and stared.

Daniel did the same for the second cell.

Melinda hovered behind them, not sure she wanted to see. Once in a lifetime was enough, wasn't it? Except, of course, she couldn't stop herself from following when Boyd took a step inside the tiny room.

There'd never been any furnishings except a mattress on the floor that the CSI team had hauled away. Two of the four walls were concrete, as was the floor. Dorrance had constructed the other two walls of cinder blocks made permanent with masonry. The doors were steel.

Maybe, she thought, the women *hadn't* been able to hear that squeaky stair. Maybe they'd had no warning at all of his visits.

The smell…she didn't know, but the beam of her light found those rusty stains. Most were on the floor, but Andrea had said that she'd completely broken at one point and hammered and clawed at the walls until her hands were raw and fingers broken. Melinda's stomach rolled at the sight in front of her tangled with memories.

Even deeply shadowed, the expression on Boyd's face was unutterably grim. "He should have fried. If anyone had showed the governor a picture of either of the women and these cells, surely even he wouldn't have signed that pardon."

"All it would have taken was a little imagination." Melinda knew her voice sounded arid, all her emotions wanting to go into deep freeze. Aware of his eyes on her, she backed into the hall and went up the stairs. She'd seen enough. Coming along on this little expedition had been a mistake, now that she knew another woman was being held somewhere nearby in a space that might be as bleak, her circumstances as brutal and hopeless.

Without turning her head again, Melinda marched out the front door and straight to Boyd's Granger County vehicle. The two men joined her not more than a couple of minutes later. Nobody said a word.

Chapter Seven

At the station, Daniel said, "Have you even put away your groceries, Melinda? Go home and get some rest." Then he slammed the car door and headed for his pickup in the half-empty lot behind the low, brick building.

During the short drive, Boyd's gaze had flicked constantly to the rearview mirror. He couldn't forget Melinda was sitting directly behind him. Looking at him? Fixedly staring out a side window? That wouldn't surprise him.

Now that she'd gotten out, he expected her to head for her car, too, but instead she dropped in front of his driver's-side window. Boyd lowered it.

"You have another thought?"

"I'd appreciate it if you'd back off on the protect the little woman plan." Voice steady, she held his gaze. "You've undermined me in every meeting. I don't like the implication that I can't take care of myself, especially when I know where that's coming from."

Boyd's temper fired. In a way, she was right, but mostly, she was wrong.

"I have been nothing but professional. You're hearing what you expect me to do or say instead of—"

Darkness was falling, but he could see the simmering anger on her face just fine.

"Implying that I shouldn't be part of the investigation?" she fired back. "That the *men* can handle it better?"

Yeah, he'd screwed up once upon a time, but he couldn't believe she held on to a grudge enough to misread him so completely.

"I've asked questions that needed to be asked. Being granted that warrant was a minor miracle, and you know it. I also think you embroidered on your observations because you knew what you'd seen wasn't enough." When her mouth opened, he held up a hand. "That's not a criticism. You took a big risk, but it paid off. If you'd actually been listening to me these past few days, you'd have heard me say you're observant, smart and have a kind of insight most people don't. I've asked repeatedly what you thought, what were your best guesses. That's not undermining you."

Her mouth had closed, opened again and closed. Finally she said, "But you still think I should go into hiding. Because I'm a woman."

He rolled his shoulders. "You're a good cop."

"As if you're any judge," she snapped.

He raised his eyebrows and saw a flush rise in her cheeks.

"You're right. I want you out of this. You're dangling yourself out there like bait. Communications, my ass! Dorrance has already pinned his target on

you. Because he blames you the most for his downfall? Because he resents that it was a woman who
brought him down? Who knows. It doesn't even matter, because he doesn't just want to kill you. He wants
you under his control, he wants to rape you and hurt
you. He wants to shave your head and send us your
hair!" Somehow, his voice had risen to a roar. "Do
you know what that would do to everyone in this department? To me?"

And, God, he shouldn't have said that, because
the shock on her face morphed into astonishment.

"You?" she whispered. "There's no reason—"

"There is, and you know it." He made himself
look away from her and do some deep breathing. He
hadn't meant to say any of this, was angry at himself
for letting it get personal.

But it was. Damn it, it *was*.

"Daniel's right," he said, having regained outward calm. "You need to get some rest. I'll follow
you home."

"You don't have to—"

"I do."

She had to see he wasn't going to yield, not on this.
After a moment, she gave a stiff nod and walked away.

And yeah, she inspected the inside of her Subaru
carefully before she unlocked the door and got in.

Boyd just wished Dorrance *would* try to tail her
tonight.

MELINDA HATED FEELING FOOLISH, and how could she
not? Boyd was right—she had waited to catch him

showing what a sexist jerk he could be, and she'd called him on it without justification.

Her cheeks burned in humiliation.

She hated even more having to creep through her own house, weapon drawn, flinging open closet doors expecting the monster to jump out, peering under her bed and even in the kneehole beneath her massive antique desk. Oh, and checking window locks while well aware how quickly Dorrance could tap a hole in the glass, just as Alvarez had done at Officer Jonas's house, unlock the window and jump inside.

Fine. She'd be ready to blow a hole in him by the time he reached her bedroom.

Unless—God—he somehow masked the sound of breaking glass. Taped a pane, say, before removing it. Or waited until the neighbor's irritating rooster crowed at daybreak or provided a distraction all his own. A firecracker out front while he went in the back, say. Set on the outskirts of town, her small house sat on almost a half acre, and some of the neighbors owned even larger lots. She'd *liked* the sense of space, but now, even when confident she was alone in her house, she felt a crawling awareness of the dark landscape outside. For the first time since she'd completed the police academy, she drew every blind and set of curtains, and turned on most of the lights, too.

Then she put away her groceries, discovered that her stomach felt hollow but that the idea of eating nauseated her, and sat down at the kitchen table with a moan.

What had she been thinking to accuse Boyd of…

what? Being overprotective? Or maliciously trying to damage her standing in the department? Either of which implied that she believed he still cared about her more than two years after they'd broken off their brief relationship.

Except…*he'd* implied that he did.

She tried to shake that off. Given Dorrance's interest in her, Boyd would have insisted on following her home even if they'd been strangers when she called to drag him into this manhunt. She would have done the same for a fellow officer who was, to use Boyd's words, in Dorrance's crosshairs.

She might even be encouraging that fictional officer to go into hiding. But that other person wasn't her. Dorrance was her worst nightmare brought back to life, and she couldn't back away and still be able to live with herself.

She moaned again, her thoughts reverting to Boyd. She almost had to apologize, which meant swallowing another dose of crow. But…had he meant it, that he'd be devastated if she were attacked or even killed? And if he did…why? Had she hurt him when she walked out on him?

All she had to do was close her eyes to picture the moment he said, "This is serious. You and me."

They'd spent an astonishing night in his giant bed upstairs in his enormous log home set in the middle of thousands of acres of ranchland. After tender morning lovemaking, they'd gone down to the kitchen, both starved since they'd forgotten all about the steaks he'd been going to grill the evening before.

Boyd had been cracking eggs into a bowl while she sliced a loaf of homemade bread when he looked over his shoulder and made his pronouncement.

Melinda made a sound now, as she sat in her own deserted kitchen remembering the burst of happiness. She'd never felt anything like that before. She hadn't known she *could* fall in love with a man so completely, so fast. Seeing the tenderness and heat in his eyes, she had let herself believe in the possibility of something she had never imagined happening for her. He'd coaxed her into opening up that night, to the point where she'd told him about her youth, her sister. Explained why she'd gone into law enforcement.

But that morning, her happiness hadn't even crested when he said, "Here's the thing, though. I can't deal with you being a cop," and *poof,* all that hope and belief blinked out of existence.

She'd said, "What?" Maybe whispered it. Because she could have misheard him, couldn't she? Or misunderstood what he was asking for.

Which suggested the *poof* hadn't wiped out all her foolishly unrealistic emotions quite as fast as she wanted to think it had.

But he took care of that, explaining that he couldn't have a girlfriend who carried a gun and risked being shot on an everyday basis. He had no problem with her *working,* he'd added, but not in a dangerous career like law enforcement...

She had stared at him for what felt like ages, as if she was clicking the shutter on a camera, collecting images for a future that would not include him. Then she said something like, "I'm sure you won't have any trouble finding that girlfriend. Thanks for a fun night, but I'm asking you to stay out of my way from now on," and left.

As far as she knew, he hadn't so much as moved by the time she let herself out of the ranch house. In that last mental picture, he'd still held an uncracked egg in his hand.

He didn't follow her and hadn't called after her to stay. That was one way of taking her seriously, if not how she'd imagined at the beginning of that scene.

They didn't come face-to-face again until he'd become county sheriff and they'd had to work together on the serial killer investigation. Then she'd had a hard time seeing past her hostility.

Tonight hadn't been quite as bad. Melinda was afraid she hadn't hidden everything she felt from Daniel, but he'd avoid comment unless she behaved so badly he had to intervene. Which wouldn't happen.

Her chest burned, and so did her eyes, but she wasn't about to cry. Whatever she'd felt for Boyd Chaney hadn't survived his request that she quit her job—and his obvious belief she'd be glad to give up her chosen career to please him, or at least to make sure he wasn't inconvenienced by any worry for her at all.

That she was as attracted to him as ever, hyper-aware of his presence whenever he was near, of the way he walked—or was it prowled?—the timbre of his deep voice, the intensity in his golden-brown eyes, well, she'd just have to live with it.

She'd made the right decision then, and he had obviously agreed, or he would have followed her. Would have at least tried to explain. But he didn't.

Which meant he had no right to pretend he cared about her, she thought, on a spark of restorative anger.

So forget him.

Except—she was beginning to think she had misread him in some ways. So far, for example, he hadn't tried to grab the limelight. In fact, he'd slunk around as much as the rest of them, doing his best to avoid the hungry reporters and cameramen. He'd once confirmed a statement the Sadler police chief had given. That was all.

Okay, fine. *And* irrelevant.

Called back to the moment, she gave herself a lecture. To do her job, she needed both food and sleep. Whether she felt like eating or not, she'd do it. She had a bad feeling that sleep was another story.

BOYD DROVE PAST the turnoff to the log house on the ranch where his partner and his wife and adopted daughter lived. Through the sparse ponderosa pine woods, Boyd could see lights shining from downstairs windows. Gabe and Trina tended to go to bed early, especially now that she was pregnant, but they were obviously still up. Boyd suppressed the temptation to go knocking on their door. They were good friends, good listeners, but his feelings for Melinda were too raw to share. If he needed backup, that would be different, but he didn't. Boyd was usually glad to see how happy his friends were, but tonight envy might taint the moment, and he'd be ashamed of that.

His own huge house—he still didn't know why he'd had it built so big—was dark. His housekeeper wouldn't have thought to leave lights on for him, given the long days at this time of year.

No reason he'd be a target for this psycho, but Boyd still watched his surroundings carefully for any hint of movement as he mounted the stairs and unlocked the front door, then flicked on lights. Maybe he should have had a security system installed when the house was built, but the need for one hadn't crossed his mind. Terrorists he'd battled half a world away weren't going to follow him home.

Going into law enforcement changed the picture. You arrest enough people, you made enemies.

He wished he thought Melinda had a security system in the small house that had been more isolated than he liked to see. When they knew each other, she'd been in a rental, a duplex right in town. She'd obviously decided after their split to become a homeowner. All he'd do is feel guilty if he tried to analyze why she might have made that decision, to acquire a real home on her own.

Damn.

He'd made it to the kitchen and opened the refrigerator, not surprised to see a couple of bowls with instructions on reheating taped on top of the clear wrap.

He popped two slices of garlic bread in the toaster while the convection oven and microwave both hummed, then sat down to what had undoubtedly been green beans right out of the garden and a sizable portion of excellent lasagna. *He* hadn't had to stop at the grocery store on his way home; his housekeeper took care of that chore, along with many others.

If he hadn't panicked when he fell for Melinda, she might be sitting at the table with him right now, sharing his dinner. Except, he'd probably be even more crazed than he already was about her being the target of a nutcase.

Yeah, but she'd have had him at her side, in bed and out of it, to keep her safe, instead of her being alone in that isolated house too many miles from here.

Boyd looked down at empty dishes, not remembering having eaten beyond the first bite or two and let out a growl. There was a good reason he couldn't love a woman who thought nothing of risking her life, and he shouldn't forget that.

That was when his phone rang. He'd left it on the kitchen counter, as far away as he ever let it get. Knowing any of his ranch employees would probably call Gabe or Leon first, Boyd felt a cold clutch of anxiety by the time he picked up the phone.

The name that showed was Miguel Cordova's.

Boyd caught the call just before it went to voice mail. "Detective?"

"My little girl is missing." Terror made the younger man's voice almost unrecognizable. "She's…

she's three. I just turned out the lights, and Maria and I stopped on the way down the hall to check on her. Her bed's empty, glass pane is cut out of the window." He was panting by now. "Somebody took her."

Dorrance took her.

"I'm on my way. Just hold on. Even Dorrance wouldn't—" Boyd faltered.

"Wouldn't he?" his detective asked, almost unintelligibly.

"I'll bring SPD in on this," Boyd said.

As he went out the door, the first number he called was Melinda's.

MELINDA DROVE AT high speed, using her lights and siren even though getting to the Cordova house five minutes faster wouldn't make any difference.

This abduction couldn't be chance, a stray predator who'd been watching for a chance to grab a child. She didn't believe that, and could tell Boyd didn't, either. Daniel was arranging to get a CSI team out here, in the unlikely event the kidnapper had never watched television and therefore hadn't worn gloves. Or, hey, he could have dropped his wallet, complete with ID, without noticing as he climbed out the window carrying the girl.

Actually, that part would have been tricky since he presumably had needed to keep a hand over her mouth to keep her from screaming. And why would he have a wallet, given that he lacked ID or credit cards to fill it?

Cordova lived only a couple of miles outside the

city limits, but the opposite direction from Melinda's own house. After killing the lights and siren, she barely slowed enough to make the turn onto a cracking concrete driveway. Boyd's big black pickup truck was the only vehicle in front of the garage. Evidently, he hadn't taken his department-issue SUV home tonight. She parked beside the pickup, circled behind his back bumper to the short walkway and stopped dead.

A tricycle sat at the foot of the porch steps. A pink tricycle, with pink ribbons that reminded Melinda of a cheerleader's pom-poms dangling from the handlebars. At the clutch of pain in her chest, she thought suddenly, Boyd was right. Why would anyone in their right mind let themselves love someone when this kind of devastation could be the result? If they never recovered Cordova's kid, or found her dead, his wife would always know this happened because of his job. How could she put someone else through this?

Compartmentalize, she ordered herself. She knew better than to let herself get too emotional when her job was to stay calm, use her head, be prepared to act on an instant's notice.

She knocked lightly, and the door swung open immediately, Boyd's big body blocking her view into the house. His face was set in hard lines but gave away some of the same horror she felt.

"Let's take a look outside first," he said tersely.

Carrying a big flashlight, he led the way. "You haven't gotten a text?"

"Not yet."

"Do you know how much I hate this guy?"

"I have never in my life hated anybody as much as Dorrance, and that's saying something."

He gave her a sidelong look, reminding her that he was the only person here in Sadler who would know what she was talking about. Mercifully, he didn't comment.

They kept their distance from the open window and the pane of glass leaning against the side. The turned soil of a flower bed right there might have given them a chance at isolating a footprint, but lawn grew right up to the concrete foundation. With the weather having been so dry, the ground was rock-hard. Still, a careless step could damage any trace evidence left by Dorrance.

Left on, the ceiling light in the bedroom illuminated a square of the grass. Melinda could see lacy white curtains pulled aside and a mobile with what she thought were unicorns.

Boyd played the flashlight beam over the window, pausing on the sill, across the siding, down to the neatly cut pane of glass. Then he muttered something under his breath and turned off the light. "I hear someone arriving."

Melinda nodded, even though he might not see her, and turned to walk back around the house. "Are they—Miguel and Maria—um, holding it together?"

"More or less. They…had already gone through some of the early phases. They ran around outside screaming Carlota's name. Knocked on neighbors' doors even though they had to know that wouldn't do any good. When I first arrived, they answered a few questions but since then... They're sitting on the sofa. Paralyzed." He was quiet long enough to have her turning her head to study his face. "They shut down," he said at last.

She nodded again, and how meaningless was that? She was glad to see the CSI van, even though she couldn't imagine they'd find anything at all.

Boyd had stepped ahead and was greeting the pair that climbed out when Melinda's phone buzzed.

Déjà vu.

He turned slowly. Melinda pulled her phone from her pocket and stared in shock at the photo: a dark-haired girl curled into a ball, her tiny hands pressed over her ears. Even so, you could see her contorted face—and her tears.

The brief line of text said, Hide and Seek.

She thrust the phone at Boyd, who stared.

"We can't let Miguel or Maria see this. It'll kill them."

"No, but...she's alive."

He lifted his head, his eyes meeting Melinda's, and she knew they were thinking the same thing.

Chapter Eight

Melinda, Boyd and the CSI tech, a twenty-something guy named Jeff Stanavitch who was apparently a computer whiz, huddled around Stanavitch's laptop, set on the Cordovas' kitchen counter. Melinda had emailed the text and photo to him so that they could study it in a larger format. Boyd was ashamed to be glad to be out of sight of the terrified parents.

Miguel's gaze had followed people as they passed through the living room, but Maria had her face pressed to his chest. He held her tight. Crumpled tissues heaped the coffee table and spilled over onto the floor.

Stanavitch spoke up. "I think she's outside. The background is blurred, but…"

Boyd leaned closer. "You're right." It was hard to make out beyond the glare of the flash. There wasn't much background visible around Carlota, anyway, most of that above her. But— "Could that be a tree trunk behind her? At first I thought it was a wall, but look at the dark line." Was that a hint of peeling around it? He always enjoyed the sight of the grove of quaking aspen growing along the creek that curved through his ranch. Not that the abducted girl would be there; it could only be accessed on horseback or ATV, which were rarely used on his property.

Intent on seeing every detail, Melinda was all but pressed against his side. "It's white." She frowned. "It could be an aspen. Their bark is really pale."

The tech mumbled to himself, then opened a new screen, typed quickly and brought up a photo of a quaking aspen. They were often found in eastern Oregon, usually along a river. Somewhere wet enough to allow them to thrive.

Boyd kept thinking about the message. Dorrance could have said something like, *Lost something?* Or *Lost and Found.* What was he saying with *Hide and Seek*?

"What if he took her as part of the game he's playing with us?" he asked. "There's no hint he's ever been interested in young children, is there?"

Melinda looked at him. "No."

"What would he want with a three-year-old?"

"The most horrible kind of revenge on Miguel? As far as we know, Guy didn't have any vulnerability like a child. What could Dorrance do but kill him?"

Stanavitch was watching both of them now, looking disturbed.

"You have a point, but…what if he did this as a vicious kind of fun?" Boyd suggested. "And a different kind of message. What if he didn't keep her? He's saying, now it's up to us to find her. He could even be watching."

Waiting to ambush them. Terrorize Miguel by stealing his kid, give him joy when he found her, then kill him.

But that thought apparently didn't cross Melinda's mind, because hope brightened her eyes. "You mean… Carlota might be close by? Is that what you're saying?"

"He could have dumped her—" He shot a glance toward the living room. Hell. He wouldn't want the kid's parents to hear him. "*Left* her anywhere," he amended. "If so, somebody else may find her. But I'm thinking this was all about saying, 'I can get into any of your houses. Take your most precious possessions. Kill you without you seeing me coming.' So why not snatch her, then leave her nearby?"

"It can't be so close she could find her way home," Stanavitch said. "Or that we could hear her crying."

"No." Damn. He shouldn't have raised anyone's hopes. Especially not Melinda's.

She hadn't blinked in so long, he couldn't remember the last time he'd seen her do it. Her eyes were stunning, making him think of a sunlit forest glade. Then, suddenly, she closed her eyes, letting out a breath, the quivering tension draining from her body. Alarmed, Boyd wrapped a supportive arm around her. She so rarely revealed her deeper emotions, but how often did she investigate a crime involving a child so young?

She didn't react to his touch, only opened her eyes and said fiercely, "We have to show this to Miguel. He might recognize the tree. If that's what this is, judging from the width of the trunk, the tree has to be an old one. I'm not that familiar with this area. I don't even know if there's water nearby. It's also possible that there could be an aspen or, I don't know, a beech that's part of somebody's landscaping."

Bright flashes were visible from the corner of Boyd's eye. The other tech was photographing the bedroom, the window and cut glass.

Melinda watched him anxiously. He was surprised she hadn't charged out to the living room and hauled Miguel by his shirt collar into the kitchen. Was she respecting the fact that this crime had been committed in his jurisdiction? Or the fact that Cordova worked for Boyd? Either way, it seemed uncharacteristic for her, especially given her dislike.

"Okay," he said reluctantly. "I'll go get him."

When Boyd stepped into the living room, Miguel turned his head as if reluctantly curious.

"Can I have a word with you?" Boyd asked quietly.

Miguel blinked a couple of times before nodding. He gently disentangled himself from his wife, stood as if he bore a two-hundred-pound pack on his shoulders and trudged to Boyd, who led him into the kitchen.

Boyd explained that Dorrance had sent a photograph of Carlota. "It's hard to look at because she's crying and probably scared."

Miguel almost leaped forward.

Boyd blocked him. "Wait. We're speculating that he could have left her somewhere for us to find. We think that's a tree in the background and are hoping it might look familiar to you."

Both Boyd and Stanavitch stepped aside to allow the detective to plant himself right in front of the laptop and stare for a long, silent moment. His throat worked; his body shook. But then he said slowly, "That's an aspen. A big one."

"That's what we thought."

"There's a stand not a quarter of a mile away, along Mustang Creek." He lunged away. "We have to go look!"

"Cordova!"

As an army officer, Boyd had perfected the art of using his voice like the crack of a whip. Even Melinda was obviously startled at the impact. Miguel stopped in his tracks, eyes wild.

"Don't say anything to Maria. If nothing comes of this, it might be worse for her."

He swallowed.

"Get a flashlight, meet us out front."

A hard nod, and he took off at a near run.

"Good try," Melinda said wryly.

Yeah, Maria would notice something was up.

Melinda got a flashlight out of her car, too, and the three set off behind the house. The day's heat lingered, and he couldn't feel any breeze. This was beginning to feel like the never-ending day.

"None of the neighbors have fences," Cordova explained, his breath coming hard as he led the way at a trot.

Once they left behind anything that could be

called a backyard, this land was mostly open and dry, a few junipers scattered among the sagebrush they had to jog around. Typical of a lot of the county. But ahead, Boyd saw the dark bulk of a grove of trees. And, yeah, the air smelled damp if he wasn't imagining things.

He swept the creek with his flashlight when they reached it and saw there wasn't much to it. A sharp bend must have resulted in something of a pool here, which explained the small grove of trees.

Again, he had to physically restrain his detective. "If we're right, we've been lured here," he said, keeping his voice low. "Is there a road close by?"

"Uh…yeah." Cordova's head turned. "There's a bridge just downstream. The road's not much, but it leads to a couple of ranches."

Damn.

Boyd had driven much of the county once he became sheriff, determined to know his territory, but there were too many roads that didn't amount to much but long driveways. The post office carriers must know the names, but there often weren't signs.

His unease crystalized.

"You two start," he said, wanting to tell them both to wait until he had a look around, but too aware of what even this brief hesitation was doing to the father of the abducted child. He was shaking like a runner held too long in the starting block. "I'm going to reconnoiter, make sure there's no handy escape vehicle parked there. Be as quiet as you can. Don't yell out your daughter's name until I give the all-clear, okay?"

"Yes. Yes!" Cordova took off.

Melinda gave Boyd a look he couldn't interpret, then trotted toward the trees.

Disquieted, Boyd realized he had to take the long way around the bend to reach that bridge. Experienced at navigating in the darkness, he turned his flashlight off. He was disturbed to see that, given the scanty lower branches on the aspens and the lack of undergrowth, the other two flashlight beams were painfully visible to him, and could probably be seen from half a mile away.

He moved as fast as he could, but it wasn't fast enough.

First he heard a startled exclamation from off to his right, then a child's cry. The ensuing silence couldn't have lasted one minute before it was split by the crack of a gunshot.

Melinda.

"CARLOTA?"

Melinda spun when she heard Cordova's voice, breaking with anguish and hope, and then a small, whimpering, "Papa?"

The child was here. Alive. Thank God. *Thank God.*

Heart swelling with gratitude, Melinda hurried toward them. Her head turned. What if Dorrance was also out here? She'd covered most of the short distance when a movement seen out of the corner of her eye worked like a cattle prod. Even as she thought, *Boyd*, she knew better. Instinct sent her flying through the air, colliding with Miguel's stockier body crouched over his daughter, sending them both crashing toward the ground.

The gunshot came while they were still in the air. Miguel hit hardest, a grunt escaping him. Melinda landed awkwardly in her attempt to avoid crushing the little girl, who started screaming.

A second shot had her scrambling to cover Carlota, even as she wished she'd worn her vest. What if that bullet had found Miguel? Somewhere in there, she'd dropped her flashlight and he must have, too, because two unmoving beams illuminated nothing but trees. Maybe the shooter hadn't realized the flashlights had flown some distance from them.

While she braced herself to take a bullet, she heard running footsteps. Help coming? No, the *thud, thud* was receding. Melinda stayed where she was, kneeling protectively over the girl, but her head hung in relief.

"Miguel? Are you all right?"

"Carlota!" He sounded frantic.

"She's fine. I'm fine."

A more distant gunshot sounded, followed by a second.

Terrified anew, she wondered whether Boyd was fine, too—or whether he was down, his intense life force gone, leaving only a shell. The vivid imagery shook her.

Two more shots rang out, then…was that the sound of a car engine?

She pushed herself to her feet. Boyd might be injured, at least, need help. Momentarily dizzy, she swayed. She didn't remember hitting her head.

At her feet, Miguel was cuddling his little girl close and crooning to her.

Melinda felt suddenly uncertain of directions now that the night was so quiet. She turned in place. No, the road had to be that way—

"Melinda!" Boyd's voice was a roar.

If she whimpered in her relief, Miguel was too occupied to hear her.

"Here!" she called back. "We're here."

Not more than a minute later, the light from Boyd's flashlight speared between ghostly pale tree boles until it settled on her.

"You're blinding me," she managed to say.

"Sorry." He lowered the beam and appeared from the darkness. "He got away. Damn it, I should have handled that differently. I *knew* better."

She had, too, Melinda realized, but had let her instincts be overruled by the idea of a distraught, possibly injured child too frightened to move. Miguel's fear had probably been contagious, too.

"Was that you shooting, or him?" she asked.

"Both," he said tersely. "If I'd had a better look at him, I'd have gotten him. I was too far away to get a good shot with a handgun. Are any of you hurt?"

"I don't think so. Miguel?" She touched his shoulder.

He lifted his face to her, his expression rapturous. "No. No."

Boyd cupped Melinda's cheek. "You're bleeding."

"Oh." She lifted her hand to explore it. "Just dirt or a rock or something. We went down pretty hard."

Boyd let out a hard breath. "At least he's a lousy shot. He was waiting here. He should have gotten one of you."

"I...saw something," Melinda said. "Movement. I tackled Miguel. The bullets may have passed right over us."

"We'll look in daylight," Boyd said gruffly. "We may be able to recover one."

"Which will tell us what?" She sounded like a cop again. Almost felt like one. That steadied her. "We know he has Guy Jonas's service weapon. That almost has to be what he fired."

"Yeah." Boyd sounded seriously unhappy. "I tried to call in a BOLO, but neither of my deputies on patrol tonight was anywhere near, and the only state patrolman in the county was even farther away."

"Did you see what Dorrance was driving?"

"A sedan, not a pickup or SUV. I tried to shoot out a tire, but the way he rocketed out of here, I missed."

And was really annoyed with himself, she diagnosed.

He seemed to shake himself. "Let's get Carlota home."

Those were magic words. Too much had gone wrong, but this much was wonderfully right.

Seeing Miguel fumbling with his phone as they started out, Boyd took it and found "Maria." It was ringing when he handed it back.

"We found her. She's fine." He ducked his head. "Say 'Mama.'"

The little girl summoned a shaky, tear-choked, "Mama?"

They all heard the scream through the phone.

"We'll be home in a minute," Miguel said.

Nobody spoke again, although Boyd reached out once and took Melinda's arm to keep her from walking right into a clump of sagebrush. Did he think that she'd suffered a head injury she wasn't acknowledging?

Maybe he had reason, she admitted to herself. She hated to say, *I don't feel so good.*

At the house, the celebration verged on hysteria—tears, then laughter and back to sobs. Stanavitch wiped away a tear as he and his partner decamped. Melinda blinked hard a few times.

Miguel was the one to suddenly straighten and step back from his wife and child. "We need to leave. Pack up right now."

Maria gaped at him.

"I agree," Boyd said. "It's not safe to stay here until we catch that—" He visibly swallowed the word that had almost escaped. "I have plenty of room at my house. You can spend the rest of the night there."

"I need to get Maria and Carlota away, then come back. I want to do my job." Miguel sounded grimly determined. "But I won't risk them."

Melinda watched Boyd, guessing that he'd feel the same. It was true that the city and county together didn't field enough law enforcement officers to maintain normal coverage and hunt for a madman. But—

"You should go, too," Melinda said suddenly. "Dorrance is going to be furious. This was so elaborate, but he failed. I don't think he'll just move on to another target."

Maria stared at her husband in alarm. "What happened?"

"He took some shots at us, but missed," Miguel told her.

A terrible cry burst from her. "You must come with us!"

His face convulsed, but he said, "I'm a cop. This is what I do. You know that."

"Go," Boyd said. "That's an order. You need to put your family first right now."

His detective stared at him, but finally nodded. "Let's pack right now."

The entire small family took off to do just that, leaving Melinda and Boyd alone in the living room. He focused on her with that familiar intensity.

"Dorrance wants you more than he wants Miguel. Miguel wasn't part of the investigation at all."

"He was SWAT at the time. One of the first in the house. He might even have taken Dorrance down. I...don't know who did."

"Did he testify at the trial?"

She shook her head, knowing where he was going.

"He's not just going around executing people. It's going to be worse than that. And *you're* his prime target."

"We'll catch him before he gets to me." Melinda wished she sounded sturdier. More certain.

His eyes drilled into hers. "I want you off his radar."

Part of her wanted the same. To run. But she was already ashamed of the way she'd let him take over tonight. All she'd done was bob her head and defer to his decisions. None of which had been *wrong*, but...

"I can't do that," she said. "I can't live with myself if I do."

He tore his gaze from hers, kneaded the back of his neck. "Leaning on other people sometimes isn't so bad, Melinda."

Her heart cramped. "How would *you* know?"

His jaw tightened. "Will you come stay at the ranch, at least? Or with Deperro and his wife?"

"Endanger her? No."

"The ranch?"

She wanted to, desperately and for the wrong reasons. "I...can't. You know I can't. Anyway, it's not exactly Fort Knox."

She wasn't surprised by his glare. He didn't like that but couldn't deny it. Two of his ranch employees had been horrifically murdered by the serial killer last year. That was different, of course; nobody had known the killer was after anyone on the ranch. Boyd had been mad as hell when he learned that his employee screening had missed so much in Howard Haycroft's background. Now, everyone would be on edge, watching for strangers and unfamiliar vehicles. Still, he couldn't promise her complete security.

"And I can't do my job if you hem me in too much," she continued. "And that's what you'll do, given half a chance. You won't be able to help yourself."

They stared at each other, the air all but crackling with the tension. Miguel interrupted the standoff, pulling a large suitcase and carrying another as he emerged from the hall. "We're almost ready. Maria is making sure she has Carlota's favorite toys."

Melinda forced a smile. "You're going home with Boyd for the night?"

"Maybe we should just start driving. He can't be watching us now."

"He could be," Boyd said quietly. "Let's not take a chance. You'll be safe at my place, and tomorrow I can escort you to the airport. The farther away you go, the better."

"Maria has family in Mexico. On the Yucatàn. We can go there."

"Good." Boyd rolled his head as if his neck ached and said, "Let me load those for you."

Minutes later they locked up, Boyd accepting a key to the house after having promised to send a ranch hand in the morning to board up the window as a temporary measure. She saw him look at her one more time, just before she got into her Subaru to join the convoy that would take them through town and out the other side. Her head still hurt, but the dizziness had been temporary, and she had no problem driving.

She flashed her headlights just before she peeled off to go home, hating the anxiety she couldn't shake, but refusing to succumb to it.

Chapter Nine

The media crowd seemed to be mushrooming by the day, even though flashing Dorrance's face everywhere had yet to produce a verifiable sighting. Heads and cameras swiveled when Boyd slowed to turn in beside the police station, but he ignored them and parked in back. Somebody had stationed a uniform to block any attempt by a cameraman or enterprising reporter to slip through to the back of the building.

Approaching the conference room inside, Boyd spotted Melinda and a man he didn't know in the hall. For a moment, he thought they were talking, but the guy went on in and she remained where she was, a phone to her ear.

"No!" she exclaimed when he got close enough to hear. Her gaze flew to his. "Don't tell me where you are!"

Eyebrows lifting, Boyd stopped a few feet from her.

"He called your father?" What looked like intense worry crinkled her forehead and she sounded urgent when she responded. "Call him. He needs to disappear for a while. Just...go stay somewhere, where he can't be traced. You need to do the same, Erica." After a pause, she said, "No, I don't really think he'll go after you. He's…occupied here in town. He seems to be stalking some of the police officers involved in his arrest. But I don't think you should take any chance at all. If he got to your dad…"

Not a possibility Boyd wanted to think about.

Melinda's back and forth with the young woman who'd been one of the victims continued for another couple of minutes, Boyd waiting it out. Melinda never looked away from him.

The same tiredness showed on her face that he'd seen on his own in the mirror this morning—dark circles under her eyes, worry lines that were at least a decade too soon. He wanted to smooth them out but felt lucky she hadn't jerked her head to order him peremptorily into the meeting room. Instead… He might be imagining it, but he thought she was drawing some strength from him.

Ending the call at last, she said, "I keep thinking Dorrance can't get any more evil and then he does. I had to work to find the dad's phone number. It's not good that Dorrance managed without my resources."

Boyd swore, then said, "We'd better get in there. It looks like our task force has grown. No point in us talking about this when everyone will want to hear about the call."

She nodded and went ahead of him, taking a single seat on the far side of the table. Boyd pulled out a chair between Alvarez, who was back, and Lieutenant Matson.

Two people he didn't know were present, just as well since Detective Cordova had gotten on a plane earlier this morning with his wife and child. From Portland, a flight would take them to Mexico City. Cordova had said they'd stay with family well outside of the city. He didn't see how anyone could find them. He'd call every few days to find out when they could safely return home.

Daniel introduced the two new participants as an FBI special agent, Alan Cabe, and a representative from the Oregon State Police Crime Analyst Unit, better known as CAU. Aaron Loftis was about Boyd's age and there to help how he could, he said calmly, no suggestion that he felt superior to the mere locals. Boyd hadn't yet had occasion to call on the services of the CAU. But he knew that most jurisdictions in Oregon were grateful for its help with everything from managing a major investigation when that was beyond the capability of a small police force, to helping process evidence, do data research, handle tip lines and analyze incoming data in a way most police had no experience doing. Some of that presumably overlapped what FBI special agent Cabe could do, but too much help was better than not enough, in Boyd's opinion.

The rest of the task force introduced themselves in turn, and then Melinda and Boyd brought everyone up to speed on the events of the past twenty-four hours, including the phone call she'd just taken. Boyd was still kicking himself for not getting into place last night to locate Dorrance before letting Cordova start searching for his daughter, but nobody else commented. The hunt for a child that young and vulnerable was fraught with emotion even when she wasn't the daughter of an officer who was part of the search for Dorrance.

Their discussion about going forward was less productive. They agreed that Loftis would take charge of the tip line information coming into both the county and SPD, categorizing and analyzing it in a way that just wasn't happening. They needed a geographic breakdown, for example—what if several people living in the same vicinity had claimed to see him? Even if their particular claims hadn't been convincing, the cluster would say something.

Matson surprised Boyd by wanting to ask the public to call to report any women they knew who lived alone and wouldn't normally be missed immediately.

Melinda jumped on that. "You know that no matter what we say, people will rush to check on neighbors rather than asking us to do it. We'd be putting them in danger."

A short discussion resulted in an agreement to hold off at least temporarily. Emmett Yates was assigned to talk to postal delivery employees, who might be able to identify some single women living in isolated homes.

Then Daniel interjected. "Who says the woman is single? Or should I say, *was* single? A retired couple would have done just as well. Dorrance wouldn't hesitate to kill the husband."

The more they talked, the higher rose the level of frustration.

The FBI agent spoke up. "Unless he's highly skilled at disguises, this Dorrance will be seen. He took a huge chance leaving the message in Detective McIntosh's car, for example. I gather it was still daylight?"

"It was," she agreed.

"It doesn't take long to lower the window enough to drop in the envelope, but that's also the kind of thing that would catch the eye of someone passing by, and traffic in and out of any major grocery store tends to be constant. Since he got by with it the once, he may be emboldened to believe he can do anything he wants."

"He got into Detective Cordova's house when the detective and his wife were both home," Boyd said, hearing his own grim tone. "Broke in and abducted their daughter without making a sound."

Special Agent Cabe leaned forward. "Again, high risk. Yes, he waited for darkness, but what if she'd been awake when he climbed in the window? She might have screamed. My point is that he could have snatched her during the day when an armed law enforcement officer wasn't a few feet away. He wanted to issue a challenge more than he wanted to go unseen."

"He expects to be killed," Melinda said slowly. "But he intends to take revenge on as many of us as possible first."

Cabe, midforties at a guess, nodded. "That's my take."

"What if we persuade every single person who played any role at all in his arrest and conviction to go into hiding?" Tom Alvarez asked.

Boyd couldn't help looking at Melinda, who narrowed her eyes at him in warning.

It was Cabe who said, "How many people are we talking? Including the defense team, prosecutor's office, the neighbor who reported him, all the cops tied to his ultimate arrest?"

"Too many," Daniel said flatly. "Do we include the paralegal? The receptionist at the law firm who put calls through to Dorrance's attorney—or claimed sometimes he wasn't available? We have to be talking about twenty-five, thirty people, *and* their families. Spouses and teenage kids who have jobs."

"So it's impractical." Cabe frowned. "If this guy was able to track down one of the two victims' fathers, I worry that he's willing to go to any length to find the people he blames most. Right now, we know he's here in town, or at least nearby. Our chances of cornering him here are better than they would be if he starts traveling."

Boyd agreed, but pointed out, "The traveling would present pitfalls for him, though. Has he come up with a driver's license that can pass scrutiny if he gets pulled over? Car registration? I doubt he can jump through the hoops to fly commercially. Does he expose himself by staying in motels, or go to the length he apparently has here to set up a hideout?"

"All true," the FBI agent agreed, "but with him on the move, we'd have to warn countless other law enforcement agencies, convince them how dangerous this man is. If we have to take this manhunt nationwide, that would increase the risk of him killing someone just because they stand in his way or spot him at a bad moment."

"An ambush might be feasible, except we still have too many potential targets who've refused to hide," Daniel commented.

Except they all knew Dorrance was fixated on one particular target. Boyd tensed, bracing himself for someone to point out that logical fact.

No one did. Partly, he assumed, because the SOB clearly wanted to enjoy first taking out other people he hated.

Daniel continued, "It's essential that we follow up at least daily with each and every one of them. We can't let someone drop from our radar."

For the most part, periodic contact was already happening. While it was reassuring that everyone on their list had been alive and well this morning, sooner or later one of them wouldn't answer the call. Chances were good that person would already be dead.

What Boyd hated most was that they had no good strings to pull to locate a man who sure as hell already had his next victim targeted—and Dorrance had to be enraged because he'd failed to kill Miguel Cordova.

MELINDA WISHED THE SUN wasn't reflecting off the windows as she surveyed the weather-beaten, small house beside a grove of cottonwood trees on the out-skirts of Sadler. The detached garage was in a sorry state, missing shingles on the roof like a kid shed-ding baby teeth, the siding gray and cracking. The doors hung crookedly but were nonetheless closed. A vehicle could be hidden within.

In marginally better shape, the house obviously hadn't had a fresh coat of paint in decades, but the roof showed signs of being patched at some point. The yard was overrun with weeds, but the drive-way wasn't as it might have been if the place was deserted.

She was probably wasting her time—almost cer-tainly was—but she'd already driven several routes Dorrance could have taken between his workplace and home, then widened her search radius gradually. Boyd wouldn't approve of her so much as getting out of her car in an isolated location like this without backup, but there weren't enough of them looking to be able to double up personnel, no matter what the lieutenant had recommended. This house *could* suit a nutcase holding a woman captive, since it was far enough off the beaten track, passersby out on the road probably rarely gave it so much as a glance.

She got out, hesitated, then drew her gun be-fore she hustled to the garage. No windows. The doors were held together by a crude padlock, rust-ing enough that she could tell it hadn't been recently replaced. She pushed hard to widen the gap between the doors enough to peer in. A thin band of light let her see that the space was mostly empty. Darker shapes around the edges might be a workbench, tools like a mower and Weedwacker or a pile of boxes.

She tipped her head and listened, but all she heard was a distant whine of a motorcycle engine accelerating. From this angle, the sun's reflection wasn't blinding her when she looked at the house, but several windows were covered by roller shades or curtains. She trotted up to the porch, positioned herself well to one side of the front door before knocking on it firmly.

Now the silence was complete.

Until a small *ding* came from her pocket. A text. Her heart jumped even as she knew the text was likely from Boyd or Daniel or another cop. Or even a friend. She did have some of those.

Melinda pressed her back to the house wall beside the front door as she pulled the phone from her pocket and lifted it. A photo appeared. She had to blink a couple of times to make out what she was looking at. When she succeeded, bile rose into her throat.

Oh, God, oh, God.

Daniel. She should call Daniel first, but her thumb found Boyd's name instead.

Even as she listened to the ringing, she hoped no one was home here. If someone suddenly opened that door, she might have a heart attack—or shoot before she knew who she was looking at.

SHE MET BOYD and Daniel at Mack Humrich's house. Melinda was the first there, but she waited in her car until two more vehicles arrived. Even then, she was so reluctant to get out and join the two men, she felt as if she were moving against resistance when she forced herself out of the car.

Daniel spoke first. "We can't be sure his body is here."

He didn't want to go looking either, she realized.

A fellow SPD officer, Mack had been a SWAT team member and had served on a regional task force aiming to prevent drug trafficking. He was a good cop. Melinda had known him well. They'd even dated a few times years ago, before she'd come to her senses and realized that they'd screw up a good working relationship. He hadn't seemed to disagree, and as far as she could tell, there'd been no hard feelings on either side.

She'd give a lot to be able to believe that the dead man in the photo was someone else, anyone else, but she'd known him the minute her eyes really focused.

Boyd was watching her, so she squared her shoulders and said, "Looks like the side door into the garage is standing open."

Both men nodded. Still none of them moved.

"Is he married?" Boyd asked. "Does he have kids?"

"No kids." Thank God. "He's married, but, um, I heard they've been having problems. They might be separated. I haven't seen him to talk to in several months."

Daniel sighed. "Me either. He's been on nights."

"We going to do this?" Boyd asked.

"I requested backup." Daniel turned his head at

the sound of another car. "This could be another ambush."

Broad daylight, at least three cops present, Melinda doubted it. Plus, of the three of them, *she* was the only target that would interest Dorrance. Although she supposed he might not mind mowing down other, random cops at this point.

Joined by two uniformed patrol officers, they all pulled their weapons and spread out to circle the house and garage. She was able to catch a glimpse inside the garage from that open door but didn't see anyone, living or dead.

She smelled the recently dead, though, which further sickened her.

Boyd reported finding the sliding door at the back of the house unlocked. He and the two uniforms did a search while Daniel and Melinda looked at each other, then burst into the garage crying, "Police!"

No one was there except the body hanging from the rafters. Melinda went outside, ducked around to the back of the garage and lost her lunch.

She was wiping her lips, grateful to see a faucet she could use to rinse her mouth, when Boyd appeared. He was the last person she would have wanted to see her so distraught she was puking.

"Don't say anything," she told him, stony.

He looked genuinely surprised as well as concerned for her. "What would I say? I know you've seen as bad or worse than this and worked through it." A nerve twitched under his eye. "It's…harder when you know someone. Worse yet when he was a friend."

She heard a question in that. Gentle, not a demand for information, so she nodded and heard herself say, "We dated a few times, seven or eight years ago. It didn't go very far. Both of us were more focused on our careers, but—" her mouth tasted foul "—you're right. It's different than seeing the victims of that serial killer, even though he'd done such horrible things to them."

She saw nothing but kindness on his face. Even… tenderness? Surely not from Boyd Chaney!

"Better rinse out your mouth and splash some water on your face so we can get back to work."

Melinda nodded, crouched in front of the faucet and turned on the water. When she'd finished rinsing out her mouth, Boyd's big hand appeared in front of her, offering a roll of mints.

She popped two into her mouth and handed the roll back to him. Making herself rise to her feet was hard, but she did it.

Furrows had formed between Boyd's dark eyebrows. "This is a lot more barbaric than Jonas's murder."

"Because he's mad about yesterday's disaster?" she suggested.

His gaze searched her face. "Is there any way he could know this Humrich and you were more than fellow officers?"

Just like that, she wanted to puke again. Instead, she stared at Boyd in shock. What if Mack had suffered so terribly only because Dorrance wanted to upset her?

"I don't see how," she said in a thin voice.

"Were you dating him when the raid happened?"

"I...don't remember." She closed her eyes. Yes, she did. She and Mack had exchanged a fraught glance as she descended into the basement. "Yes," she whispered. "Even so..."

"Someone at Dorrance's law firm might have found out. Thought the relationship could be used to discredit you in some way." He made a raw sound and reached for her. "Damn it, Melinda! This is *not* your fault. You know that. The guy is a sicko."

A few days before, she couldn't have imagined a circumstance that would have had her willingly leaning into this man's embrace, but right this minute, she laid her cheek against his powerful chest and tried to soak in the strength of his arms wrapped around her.

"What happened to Mack may not be my fault," she mumbled into Boyd's solid chest, "but it's because of me."

His arms tightened. The rumble she felt in his chest had to be a kind of growl. "No," he said.

"Yes."

Chapter Ten

At the end of the day, the task force members split up to go their separate ways. Nobody suggested stopping for a meal together, even though most of them probably hadn't had lunch. Melinda, for one, had zero appetite. Daniel probably just wanted to get home to Lindsay, the lieutenant to his wife. Alvarez was married, too, and probably both the FBI agent and Aaron Loftis, the guy borrowed from the Oregon State Police Crime Analysis Unit.

Boyd…didn't say anything, just nodded, got into his SUV and drove away. In fact, he was the first to go. She couldn't quite decipher his last glance at her.

Fifteen minutes later, Melinda entered her own house with her weapon drawn and did what was beginning to be a standard search before she could relax at all. Then, after removing her holster and badge, she poured herself a glass of wine. Figuring her paranoia was justified, she kept the semiautomatic close, lying on the sofa beside her.

Although the TV remote control was at hand, too, she didn't reach for it. A little later, she'd watch the local news, see what the chief had said about the latest murder and how he handled the increasingly hysterical questions, but otherwise had no interest in entertainment or national or international crises. Instead, she stared at the dark television screen and saw Mack's body. Somebody must have called his wife, she thought. Matson, maybe?

Suddenly, what she saw instead was Boyd's face when he'd followed her behind the garage. She hadn't known he could look so gentle, or that he'd understand her shock and grief.

I should have, she realized. Of course, he'd have seen good friends die in awful ways. For the first time, it occurred to her that his desire to hire ex-army rangers to work on his ranch wasn't entirely because he preferred having like-minded buddies around— or warriors ready to spring into action when called. Rather, the presence of those men might be a comfort—they had all had the same kind of experiences, they understood each other, they might even *need* each other on occasion.

She wrinkled her nose. If any of them were ever willing to expose raw emotions.

And yet he'd accepted her doing so. Because she was a woman? Melinda tried to work up some temper but failed because she truly believed he'd have acted the same if it had been Daniel who'd just lost a good friend.

Maybe she'd jumped to conclusions about Boyd that just weren't accurate.

Melinda examined that thought for a moment but

didn't know where to go with it. She'd shut the door on their relationship. Since he hadn't contacted her since, there was no reason to think he might still harbor any special feelings for her. If he'd gotten married during the interval, she was sure she'd have heard, but he might well have a live-in companion. Could be that's why he'd left without a word, probably as relieved to be heading home as Daniel had to be.

She shook her head. Forget Boyd. Who she needed to be thinking about was Dorrance. Where he was, what he was planning, how they could stop him before he destroyed any more lives.

NOT A BIG FAN of fast food, Boyd still used the drive-through at a burger joint to load up on provisions of a sort, then navigated through town to Lieutenant Edward Matson's house.

What he wanted to do—hell, not *wanted*—what he was damn near desperate to do—was stake out Melinda's house. Watch over her. But he'd had an uneasy feeling that had become needle sharp today. Then-detective Ed Matson had been primary once Melinda persuaded the department to investigate Gene Dorrance. He could have taken a cursory look and said, *Yeah, this is a waste of my time.* He didn't. Ultimately, *he* was responsible for calling in SWAT, going ahead with the raid that brought down Dorrance. *He* was a logical next target, given that the partner he'd worked with at the time had retired and moved away, placing himself out of immediate reach.

Since the beginning, everyone had watched Melinda out of the corners of their eyes—and yes, that was probably because she was female and, in their heart of hearts, deemed less able to take care of herself, and also, of course, because she was the person Dorrance had chosen to communicate with. What nobody seemed to remember was that Matson was near retirement. He did still appear fit, but Boyd had noticed a stiffness in the way he rose from chairs or got in or out of his vehicle, maybe because he didn't want anyone to know he had back problems or the like. Was he still a regular at the range? Mostly administrative now, when had he last pulled his weapon on the job?

Boyd hated the idea of Melinda having to face down Dorrance, but he had more faith in her reaction time and skill than he did in Matson's. Thus his plan for tonight. The lieutenant wouldn't like being perceived as weak any more than Melinda would, but Boyd didn't intend to be seen—unless something happened.

Never having needed a lot of sleep, he figured to find a good place to keep an eye on Matson's house and settle in for the night. His extensive combat experience meant he could snatch a little shut-eye but be awake and alert at the slightest sound or movement. Once they caught this scumbag, he'd have plenty of time to catch up on sleep.

Turned out the Matsons' house was a standard rambler on a normal size city lot. Garages were in back of the houses in this neighborhood, accessed via an alley.

Boyd drove in a slow circle around the block, automatically noting parked cars, heavy shrubbery, the two backyards enclosed by six-foot-high board fences. Fortunately, neither of those bordered Matson's backyard, which was neatly mowed and included a couple of fruit trees and some raised garden beds filled with thriving rows of plants.

If he were the one planning to penetrate the house or make an attack when the lieutenant was arriving or departing, he'd set up or approach from the back. The front was too open, and once darkness fell would be lit by streetlamps at each end of the block as well as any porch lights left on. Anybody glancing out a front window would pay attention to a man cutting across a yard, too.

One real problem: the bulk of the garage would hide an intruder coming from the opposite direction, or that someone could hide behind any of several other garages or inside the fence of the yard just behind the Matson's. Boyd could call for someone to join him, but what was really just an uneasy feeling didn't seem to justify asking anyone else to spend the night on watch, too.

He'd parked on the cross street and walked down the alley when he saw the lieutenant's car turn in. Stepping behind a hedge, he watched as the garage door rose and Matson drove into it, not noticing Boyd. Not impressed, Boyd could only hope the guy had at least taken a good look to be sure no one was waiting inside for him before he pushed the button to close the door, shutting himself in.

There was no other movement up or down the alley. Boyd moved to a position that let him watch as the lieutenant came out of his garage, crossed his yard and let himself into his house—through a door with a big glass pane that made even a dead-bolt lock useless. The same kind Jonas had had. Boyd shook his head. These were cops. They had to know better.

He settled between the garage and a big lilac shrub to eat his dinner. Once darkness cloaked him, he began hourly circuits that took in much of the block. He did manage a few naps, and woke because he'd set an internal clock, not because he'd been startled awake.

He carried his phone, but it didn't once vibrate during the night.

Boyd decided that after he'd followed Matson into work, he'd stay in his own vehicle to make his daily checks on potential targets before going into the station himself to join the task force meeting.

When a light went on in what was likely Matson's bedroom, Boyd stretched muscles and sharpened his surveillance. He wished the lieutenant didn't have to walk across the yard to reach the garage, making himself a perfect target. Boyd was also less than happy because he couldn't be as close as he should be without being seen. He could cover one side of the garage or the other, not both. Dorrance had fired some shots the other night, which meant he was carrying Officer Jonas's gun. He probably wasn't all that accurate, but that didn't matter if he could get close enough. So far, he'd fired the Glock only four times that they knew about, leaving plenty of bullets without him needing to shop for ammunition.

The kitchen light came on. Dawn brightened the sky, bringing into focus the landscaping in the yard, the lines of the clapboard on the house and garage. Boyd heard a few car engines as he waited, natural since early birds would be heading into work. He couldn't always tell where those sounds came from.

The back door opened a lot sooner than Boyd had expected. Matson couldn't possibly have eaten breakfast. Had he even gulped a cup of coffee? He paused on the small deck, looking from one side to the other in suspicion before unsnapping his holster and resting his hand on the butt of his service weapon while taking the step down to the grass. Not completely unaware of his danger, then.

Boyd crouched behind some shrub he couldn't identify, the only spot in the yard that allowed him to watch Matson cross all the way to the back door into the garage. What he couldn't see was around the corner of the damn structure—and he'd have to hustle to get eyes on the alley when the lieutenant backed out into it.

Matson was two steps from the door, hand outstretched with keys held in it, when movement erupted beyond him. A gun barked before the lieutenant could turn or unholster his own weapon. Time seemed to slow for Boyd, until he was seeing something like a slide show.

Black-clad man with his face covered. Gun extended in a double-handed grip.

Boyd shouted. Another shot, another. Matson falling. The assailant's head turning toward him.

Boyd running and firing simultaneously. Something burned his arm. Dorrance staggering against the garage, clutching at his shoulder or chest. Whirling around the corner.

Back door of the house opening.

Boyd yelled, "Stay inside!" and tore past the fallen man to circle the garage in pursuit of the *slap*, *slap* of footsteps in the alley. By the time Boyd reached it, he couldn't see anyone. He ran full out but heard an engine start and tires squeal before he reached the street. A charcoal-gray sedan turned the corner and went out of sight.

Despite gasping for breath, Boyd swore creatively. He might have had a chance of catching the murdering bastard if he'd parked at this side of the block, but he hadn't.

Holstering his weapon, he jogged back the way he'd come, calling 911 as he went.

The moment the dispatcher answered, he demanded an ambulance and gave the address. "Injured man is in the backyard." He described the car, guessed at make and model and asked for all available units to watch for it.

"I'll call Sergeant Deperro myself," he said, just as he came around the garage.

The woman pressing what looked like dish towels to Matson's chest had to be his wife. Her expression distraught, she was almost screaming, "Ed. Ed! You're going to be fine. I know you are. You *have* to be." She lifted her head, her wild eyes finding Boyd and focusing on the phone he still held. "Sheriff? Please. Please! Call—"

He interrupted. "Ambulance is on the way." He dropped to his knees beside the lieutenant. "Let me take a look."

That look wasn't reassuring. Matson still had a pulse, but given the amount of blood he was losing, he wouldn't for long.

Boyd tore his long-sleeve T-shirt over his head and applied it to one of the wounds while Mrs. Matson pressed the already saturated kitchen towels to her husband's side.

He heard one siren, then another. When the medics appeared at a run, Boyd kept his hand in place until a gloved one wielding dressings replaced it. Then he gently drew the lieutenant's wife back.

"Give them room to work."

Sobbing, she let him help her to her feet. Still, her head turned until she couldn't see her husband anymore.

Frantically, she pulled away from him. "I have to get to the hospital."

"I'll drive you. I'll meet you out in front once you've grabbed your purse or anything else you need."

She swiped at her wet face and blinked a few times. "You're hurt, too."

"What?"

"Your arm."

He glanced down dismissively, remembering the burn across his upper arm. He'd felt that before. "I'll have it checked out when we get to the hospital."

Another sob broke from her. She spun and raced into the house. Boyd went to get his SUV, hoping he'd left another T-shirt or windbreaker in it.

MELINDA MADE HERSELF slow to a walk when she reached the double glass doors into the emergency room, even though she was scared down to her core.

Daniel's call had caught her as she was leaving her house. She'd instantly lost all sense of caution, dashing to her Subaru without taking any precautions, and broke speed limits getting to the hospital. Thank heavens there'd been one empty slot remaining for a law enforcement vehicle, saving her from having to hunt for a parking place.

She immediately saw Daniel talking to a man in a green scrub top. The two stood near the doors leading to the back. Her gaze locked on the guy in scrubs. Boyd. A thick bandage wrapped his powerful upper arm.

So close, she thought, almost numbly. He could have been killed. Freaked beyond common sense— he was right there in front of her, for Pete's sake, *alive*—she fought to hide a reaction that was totally out of proportion.

As she walked toward them, both men turned. Boyd's gaze was penetrating.

"How's Lieutenant Matson?" she asked.

"In surgery. We were just waiting for you. Let's go on up," Daniel said.

She nodded, holding back any other questions until they were in an elevator that they had to themselves.

"He shot you."

Boyd grimaced. "Not much more than a graze. Cut through some muscle, that's all."

That's all.

Melinda swallowed. "Will you tell me—" The elevator doors opened.

They found the lieutenant's wife in a waiting room. She was surrounded by family and friends. Melinda had met Matson's son before but not his daughter and exchanged nods with him. Then the three cops retreated to another, small waiting room where they could speak freely.

Boyd told her what happened more tersely than she'd have liked, but she could fill in the blanks. He was mad at himself, she realized, feeling as if he should have prevented the attack or killed or captured Dorrance.

Frowning, she asked, "What were you doing there?"

Daniel said, "Took the words out of my mouth."

"Just seemed logical the lieutenant could be a next target." Seeing Melinda's mouth open, Boyd said, "Yeah, I know he's a cop, but it's my impression he mostly rides a desk these days. I wondered if he'd react quick enough to a threat."

"And he didn't," she said bleakly.

"He didn't get much warning. He had his hand

on his gun but didn't get a chance to draw it. I was too far away."

There was that tone again. Yep, he believed he'd screwed up.

"Lieutenant Matson would be dead for sure if you hadn't been there," she reminded him.

A stark look in his golden-brown eyes, he met her gaze. "He took three bullets. He lost a lot of blood."

Chilled, she couldn't mistake what he was saying: Matson was in critical condition. He might not make it through the surgery.

"You think you wounded Dorrance?"

"I hit him in the left shoulder." He touched the spot on his own body. "Couldn't have done a lot of damage, though, or he wouldn't have been able to run so fast."

He scrolled through photographs that showed car makes from the rear, and finally shook his head. "Older Camry is my best guess, but I'm not sure."

Daniel had already notified not only the ER here at the hospital, but also urgent care clinics and other hospitals in this and neighboring counties.

"Doubt he'd dare try to get medical care," Daniel said, "but you might have done more damage than you think you did. Adrenaline can disguise symptoms for a while."

The men exchanged a look, and Melinda knew they'd both experienced the phenomenon while in combat.

An hour passed, then another. They took turns making calls and also checking on Mrs. Matson.

Otherwise, silence prevailed. Melinda's gaze strayed frequently to Boyd. This time, he was leaning forward in the chair, elbows braced on his knees, head hanging. Did he hurt worse than he'd admit to? she couldn't help wondering.

"I hear voices." She popped to her feet.

The men rose too, and followed her down the short hall to the larger waiting room. A surgeon with his mask pulled below his chin was indeed there.

"…next hours," Melinda heard him say.

As he retreated, Daniel stopped him in the hall for a repeat of what he'd told the family. Judging from what she'd heard from Boyd, nothing about what the surgeon said was a surprise. Melinda had the impression he was being more honest with them than he'd been with the family. That the lieutenant had made it through the surgery was a positive, but he was still at high risk of dying.

As her gaze followed the surgeon walking away, Melinda clenched her teeth. "I want to kill Gene Dorrance," she heard herself blurt.

Blistering anger showed on Daniel's face. "You're not alone. I've never hoped before that I had to shoot someone," he growled.

Boyd's expression gave nothing away, even though he was the only one of them who'd actually had a chance to bring down Dorrance.

He only said, "He's a monster, but the right tip will come in. Someone is going to spot him. Sooner or later, it has to happen."

Melinda wanted to think the same, but so far Dorrance had appeared and disappeared with remarkable ease, leaving them falling on their faces in his wake.

An emotion deeper, more despairing, accompanied the anger. Feeling it swell in her chest until it all but choked her, she turned her back to the men. "The lieutenant has been really good to me. If he doesn't make it—" She couldn't finish.

A big hand squeezed her shoulder. Boyd's hand, the touch speaking for him.

Chapter Eleven

Two days later—days during which Dorrance made no move, calls to the tip lines declined and Ed Matson remained in critical condition—Boyd struggled to rein in his frustration. In the past week, he hadn't had time to so much as saddle a horse, much less actually take a ride. If his partner, Gabe Decker, hadn't accepted medical retirement from the rangers and stepped in here on the ranch, Boyd knew he couldn't possibly have run for sheriff. Truthfully, guilt still surfaced even though he was consumed by current events and his fear for Melinda, a woman who'd never admit to being afraid for herself. But, damn, he'd never realized how much he'd have to dump on Gabe.

Not that Gabe was complaining. He and his psychologist wife, Trina, had had dinner with Boyd last night. Their five-year-old adoptive daughter was away for a week, staying with her grandmother. Boyd had a bad feeling that Gabe saw right through him and knew what a big part Melinda played in his turmoil.

And maybe not just Gabe, Boyd thought uneasily. Trina was unnervingly perceptive, enough to have scared the hell out of Gabe when they first met. Boyd suspected that she was now intrigued by his own all-too-visible tension, a contrast to his usual laid-back style.

Gabe told him, "You had sole responsibility for the ranch for three years before I joined you. You did fine. I'll do fine, too. If I could help you find that piece of—" He'd glanced at his wife. "You have to know I'd be on board."

All of which was true.

Still brooding, Boyd shouldered his way into the sheriff's department headquarters, nodded at the receptionist and stalked toward his office.

He hadn't reached it when his newest hire—and the first female deputy in this county—leaned out of the squad room.

"Sheriff?" She sounded urgent. "Jerry—" She flushed. "I mean, Deputy Miller says he has a woman on the line he thinks you should talk to."

He'd like to feel hopeful, but a lot of ultimately useless callers had been forwarded to him, and undoubtedly the same was true over at the Sadler PD. Hell, the FBI, the Oregon State Police and, who knew, maybe the police departments on the other side of the state were probably all fielding equally useless calls. Still, a minute later he was at his desk and picking up his phone.

"Ma'am, this is Sheriff Chaney. I hate to ask you to start all over, but I'm afraid I need to."

She introduced herself as Sherry Williams and told him her husband had had a stroke and died four months before. "He was only fifty-four." Quiet for a minute she resumed. "One of our neighbors is a retired nurse. Maybe sixty years old? We always smiled and said hello at the mailbox—you know what that's like—but for most of that time she was still working, too, and not at all the same hours as I was. Neither of us suggested getting together for so much as coffee. But after Ron died, she brought over a casserole and sat down to talk to me. Her husband died ten years ago, you see, and suddenly, like Ron did. I don't know if it would be better to have some warning, or not— Oh, I'm getting off track. Anyway, I found out that a lot of my friends didn't know what to say to me, but Kristina did."

"Kristina?"

"Morgan. Kristina Morgan."

Boyd jotted it on a notepad. This story was pushing all the right buttons.

"Well, my sister came to stay and I saw less of Kristina, and then I had to go back to work…" She trailed off. "I feel awful about it now, but we haven't talked in, oh, at least a couple of weeks. I've left several recent messages, and she hasn't called back. I thought she might be away, or maybe not interested in a long-term friendship—it seemed like she didn't go out much or have people over. You know."

In other words, a loner.

"I haven't seen her either, not even to wave to. I guess that's why I thought she might be away. And

I can't see her house from mine. Ron and I—" She swallowed. "I have a couple of acres, and I'm pretty sure Kristina does, too. The land is scrubby, with a bunch of junipers."

When she didn't continue, Boyd asked, "What prompted you to call now?"

"Oh! I should have said! Well, to start with, I just didn't follow the news after I lost Ron. It's all so bad! I felt low enough without immersing myself in everybody else's tragedies. But the other day, I heard some people talking at work, so I did watch the local news. I kept thinking how unlikely it is that the police chief could have been talking about Kristina, but then, well, this morning I saw an unfamiliar man pulling out of her driveway."

"What was he driving?"

"Kristina's Camry. That's what was so strange."

"Did he see you?" Boyd asked with some urgency.

"I don't think so."

"Please don't make any further attempt to contact Ms. Morgan until we can do a welfare check," he said sternly.

"You'll do it soon?"

"We will. I promise."

He extracted a promise from her that she'd stay away from the neighbor's property.

He also learned that, while she hadn't gotten a good look at the man, what she saw could be a match for the photos Boyd had seen of Dorrance.

She'd called the sheriff's department because her home and Kristina Morgan's were outside the Sadler

city limits. Once he had her address and the address
for her neighbor, he promised to keep Mrs. Williams
informed.

Then he called Daniel, wishing he could keep
Melinda out of what was almost certain to be a raid.

MELINDA HUDDLED with Daniel, Emmett Yates, FBI
special agent Alan Cabe and Alex Reyes, the SWAT
lieutenant near what they'd guessed to be the property line. The rest of the team waited behind them in
silence. Boyd had secured a warrant based on Sherry
Williams's testimony, and now he'd slipped through
the thicket of junipers to do the initial reconnaissance
on the neighboring house.

She'd never particularly hankered to join SWAT,
but Melinda stewed nonetheless because both Boyd
and Daniel planned to go in with them despite not
currently being members of the team. She'd vaguely
known that Daniel had been SWAT in Portland, Oregon, while Boyd had certainly served on the military equivalent.

Boyd materialized through the scratchy foliage.
"Can't see a car," he reported. "There's a detached
double-car garage, but I can't get close enough to
look in it without taking the risk of being seen."

Daniel's face was set in hard lines. "Damn, I hope
he's there."

He and the group of six other men waited while
Boyd donned some body armor, and then they forged
ahead through the low-growing, scraggly trees. Tom
Alvarez, Cabe, Emmett and Melinda trailed behind,

stopping where they were just concealed from a white-painted, two-story farmhouse. A pair of deputies had parked out on the road so that those going into the house would have a warning should Dorrance drive up.

The SWAT team with their two temporary members broke into a trot that carried them across the short distance to the house in barely a minute or two. Their approach didn't seem to have incited any movement inside or outside the house.

Their backs flattened against the wall, they exchanged hand signals and split up, rounding the corners to the front and back. Melinda lost sight of the group that went to the back, which included Boyd. Daniel led the group to the front, waving two men to check the far side of the house. Shaking their heads, they rejoined him.

He hammered on the door. "Open the door! Police!"

Following a brief moment of waiting, he tried the doorknob, then stepped back and allowed one of the others to kick it open. He would have signaled Boyd's team to go in the back simultaneously, she assumed.

Tension high, Melinda hated not being able to do anything but wait and listen for gunfire. She wanted to pace, but couldn't without going out in the open. She wasn't alone; Cabe, who had ditched his usual dark suit for flexible boots, black T-shirt and cargo pants, watched with a hard cast to his face that she hadn't seen before.

She looked down at the face of her phone. A minute passed. Another. Windows all seemed to be covered, as they'd been in Dorrance's own house. Team members would have split up, some charging upstairs, others searching the ground floor as well as for an entrance to a potential basement. She had no idea whether a house of that era was likely to have one.

Suddenly Daniel, who'd removed his helmet, came out onto the porch and gestured for them to join him.

Melinda broke into a run. When she reached the foot of the steps, she saw his face, deeply lined, his jaw set grimly.

"This is the right house," he said. "Unfortunately, Dorrance isn't here."

"The owner?"

"She is." He scrubbed a hand roughly over his face. "We need you, Melinda. I think having another woman here will help."

Dear God.

She rushed up the steps and past Daniel. Looking bleaker than she'd ever seen him, Boyd waited in the entry. He thrust what looked like a bathrobe at her.

"This way."

Taking the robe, she asked, "Is…there a basement?"

"Yes."

They reached a door that stood open. She peered down the exceptionally steep staircase, closed her eyes for an instant and took a few deep breaths, then nodded at him and took the first step. All the way down, she was conscious of him behind her even as cold, dank air that stank of human waste and despair enveloped her.

The feeling of déjà vu was overwhelming.

Melinda passed a washer and dryer to join two SWAT officers who stood outside an open door. Shock and helplessness radiated from them despite the body armor that made them seem bigger than they really were, more intimidating. She was glad they had the sensitivity to stay back.

When she entered the tiny room, she was hardly aware of anything but the woman curled into a ball in one corner, yet she still saw the stark concrete walls and floor and the bare light bulb on the ceiling. Just as at Dorrance's house, a mattress lay on the floor. A stinking bucket sat by the doorway.

Feeling sick, Melinda went to Kristina Morgan and lowered herself to her knees within touching distance.

"Kristina?" she said gently. "My name is Melinda. I'm a police officer. I know those men frightened you, but we're here to take you out of this place. I promise. Let me help you into your robe."

After a long moment, Kristina lifted her head enough to look at Melinda. Her eyes... Color didn't matter. They might have been Erica's eyes, or Andrea's. Dead, and yet filled with horror at the same time.

Hoarse voice just audible, she whispered, "Okay," and held out an arm.

Melinda slipped the sleeve of the robe over the arm, then wrapped it around her until she straightened enough to get her second arm through the other sleeve. She was painfully thin—must have been a slender woman to start with—and now bruised. From the swelling and extreme discoloration, Melinda suspected her right cheekbone and some ribs were broken. Her head had been shaved, and her lips were dry enough to crack.

Melinda had been aware of sirens outside. "Can you walk?" she asked. "An ambulance will take you to the hospital. The EMTs can carry you up—"

The woman shook her head with determination. "No. I can make it."

Melinda smiled at her. "I'll be with you all the way."

Those eyes fastened desperately on her. "To the hospital, too? I...don't have family."

"I'll stay with you," she promised. "We're here because your neighbor got worried about you. I'll bet she'll want to come, too."

"Sherry?"

"That's right."

The first tears trickled down Kristina's cheeks.

"RIDE WITH HER," Boyd said in a low voice. "I'll bring you back out here to pick up your car later."

Melinda offered him a tremulous smile before hurrying to climb into the back of the ambulance.

He couldn't seem to move until it receded down the driveway and disappeared from sight. Then he looked at Daniel, who stood beside him.

"I heard you on the phone."

Daniel swore. "That SOB saw the patrol car and took off at high speed. They pursued but lost him. The officers still don't know how. My gut says Dorrance had figured out a way to get off-road and out of sight in case anything like this ever happened."

Boyd was considerably more profane than Daniel. "He's lost his bolt-hole. He's going to be madder than ever."

"What scares the hell out of me is that he's already identified backup options."

Boyd's blood ran cold at the idea. "We have to issue a general warning. Immediately."

"Would you rather do it, or shall I ask Chief Austin to go ahead?"

"Call him. Public and press both are comfortable with him." Jurisdiction didn't matter.

Daniel made the call, keeping it terse. The tension on his face never relented.

Stowing his phone, he said, "Done. Let's walk through."

"CSI on the way?" City and county, with their limited budgets, shared the same unit.

"Van's coming up the driveway."

Boyd glanced. Sure enough.

Neither spoke more than a few words as they studied first the living room, where the remote control sat on the coffee table beside two empty beer cans, then the kitchen. Dirty dishes and pans filled the sink. Daniel did put on latex gloves and opened the cupboard beneath the sink to allow them both to see a full trash receptacle. Meat bones, empty cans and plastic containers lay on top.

"No pizza boxes or fast food," Boyd commented.

"Lucky for him, Kristina must have had a well-stocked kitchen."

Or, as someone—Melinda?—had speculated, he'd been able to order groceries to be delivered. Left on the front porch, undoubtedly.

Boyd rolled his head to loosen aching muscles. Like Melinda, he'd already hated this guy. That hate had sharpened into a lethal edge.

Daniel still had his eyes on the trash. "Plenty of DNA."

Boyd grunted in acknowledgment. The kitchen was rife with fingerprints, too, for what use they were when they already knew the perpetrator's identity.

The one bedroom on the first floor was likely Kristina's, but the bloody sweatshirt and T-shirt on the floor weren't. Boyd wanted to pick up the sweatshirt to see where the bullet hole or holes were, but really, what difference did it make? Despite setting himself up to guard Matson, he hadn't succeeded in taking down this monster.

Somewhere, Dorrance had found first aid supplies. Discarded dressings soaked with now-dry blood filled the bathroom trash can.

Kristina's purse lay on top of the dresser, where it had been rifled. Every compartment was open, unsnapped or unzipped. A small package of tissues, lip gloss, hairbrush, a somewhat tattered paperback book with a bent cover and a price sticker from a thrift store all spilled out. A wallet lay open, stripped of any bills or credit cards.

At least now they could put a stop on the bank cards.

Yeah, and Dorrance would know they'd do it.

Boyd said, "It's probably already too late, but see if you can station officers near drive-through bank machines. If he's using his head, he'll want to get as much money out as he can from any cards Ms. Morgan had."

Daniel got on the phone again.

Nothing appeared to have been touched upstairs. Probably the scumbag had opened bureau drawers and closets to be sure they were empty of anything of value, but Boyd doubted Kristina came up here for more than a cursory cleaning. The house was a lot bigger than she needed. He wondered if she'd be able to bring herself to live here again. Go down those steps into the basement to put in a load of laundry.

Boyd kept remembering the expression on Melinda's face as she'd ushered that poor woman out of the small basement room and, one slow step after another, up the stairs. A cramping ache took up residence beneath his breastbone at the memory of the patience and tenderness she'd displayed. Her heart was a lot softer than she wanted to admit.

SWAT decamped, as did Daniel and Boyd at last. They had to reorganize their manhunt and catch this creep before he got his hands on another woman— or killed another cop he blamed for his downfall.

Heading for the hospital, Boyd discovered he was gripping the steering wheel so tight, his knuckles showed white. He deliberately relaxed his hands.

He guessed he'd known for a while that he was

in love with Melinda again. No—still in love with her. More in love with her.

When mortar fire penetrated the theoretically safe compound in Afghanistan, he'd lost the only other woman he'd ever loved Guarding himself thereafter had seemed smart. He'd clung to that belief, even though now he saw that all he'd done was lose Melinda anyway, albeit not to death. If he hadn't been such a damn fool…

Yet he hated as much as ever knowing she had a dangerous job. How could he live with that?

Pulling into one of the parking slots reserved for law enforcement, close to the emergency room entrance, he grimaced.

He already was living with the knowledge that a killer had a target on Melinda, wasn't he? And, damn it, he *knew* this wasn't anything like conditions in a war zone. A rural county in Oregon like his should be relatively peaceful. Trouble was, he'd met Melinda in the middle of a local war zone, when drug traffickers were desperate enough to get into the murder business and even target a little girl who endangered their profits. Yeah, he'd had reason to be nervous about Melinda being a cop.

Then, city and county law enforcement had had to catch a serial killer last year, and now there was this sick bastard.

A part of Boyd wanted Melinda to be safely tucked up at the ranch, instead of central to this manhunt. But if she was willing to do that, she wouldn't be the woman he increasingly feared he loved till death do they part, would she?

With a groan, he climbed out of his SUV, used the fob to lock the doors and headed into the ER for the second time in a matter of days. As long as he was here, he could stop by intensive care and check on Ed Matson.

Chapter Twelve

Melinda stared straight ahead through the windshield but saw only the face of Gene Dorrance's most recent victim. "Nobody should ever have to suffer through what she did."

Boyd glanced at her. Okay, she wasn't blind to all of her surroundings. She was never not conscious of his presence.

"No," he agreed.

After displaying surprising patience, he'd persuaded her to leave the hospital at last. Sedated, Kristina hadn't been in any shape to be questioned. He'd been right; there wasn't anything more Melinda could do. Thank heavens for Sherry Williams, the neighbor, who had become fiercely protective of Kristina and clearly had no intention of leaving her alone.

"She was there when I needed her," she told Melinda privately. "If I have to take more time off from my job, I will. She doesn't have to be alone, either."

Melinda had hugged her before Sherry returned to her friend's bedside.

Now, after a pause of several minutes, Boyd said, "We could go back for your car tomorrow."

"I'd rather get it now."

Out of the corner of her eye, she saw the muscle flex in his jaw, but he only nodded. Stubble darkened that stubborn jaw. She had a fleeting moment of remembering the texture of his unshaven chin and jaw beneath her palms and fingertips.

She should have asked Daniel for a lift. Or Tom. *Any*one but Boyd. Spending time with him, *depending* on him, was dangerous in its own way.

They continued in silence for several minutes. Melinda was still oblivious to the landscape outside and to the passing traffic.

"We're no further ahead than we ever were!" she burst out at last.

A big hand covered hers, which was balled into a fist on her thigh. "We are. Did you know that Matson may be moved out of intensive care tomorrow? He's going to make it."

That was good news, but not what she was talking about, and Boyd had to know it.

"Ms. Morgan is now safely out of his hands," he continued.

She made a sound in her throat. "Physically safe. But will she be able to come back from this?"

"Yes, I think she will," Boyd said in his calm way. "He didn't have her for years. I'm impressed with her fortitude. She was determined to walk out under her own power. Maybe she has a stronger sense of self, more confidence, than the two very young women had."

"I'd like to think so," Melinda said wearily. "I didn't even ask whether the crime scene techs came up with anything useful."

"Evidence that will help to convict him. They found an empty magazine for a Glock that has Jonas's fingerprints on it. No convenient phone numbers or addresses on notepads, though."

"A map with certain locations circled?"

His mouth curved in a wry grin. "You're an optimist. Who knew?"

Melinda snorted. That was the last word she could ever apply to herself.

Boyd flicked on the turn signal, and started up a long gravel driveway she recognized. Her Subaru sat alone where she'd parked beside Sherry Williams's garage.

Melinda squared her shoulders. "Thanks for the lift. I'll see you in the morning for the meeting?"

He braked in front of the garage. "You'll see me in your rearview mirror all the way home."

"What?" She swiveled in her seat to stare at the big man beside her. Operating on automatic, she opened her mouth to say, *I'm a cop! I don't need a protective detail!*

Except…she wasn't foolish. Lieutenant Matson would have said the same, wouldn't he?

Boyd was frowning at her. "Dorrance is on the loose, and he's seriously angry. You notice he didn't contact you after he attacked the lieutenant, and not today, either."

"Because both were failures."

"That's right. He blames everything else on you, so why not his current frustration, too?"

"I'd like to think he doesn't know where I live."

"You're not that naive."

No, she wasn't. How had Dorrance known where Miguel lived? Lieutenant Matson? Officer Jonas? Reality was that keeping your name out of a phone book didn't cut it anymore. There was too much information online.

"I want to see you safely in the house," Boyd continued inexorably, his jaw set in a way the men he'd commanded in places like Afghanistan and Iraq would probably recognize.

And truthfully...wouldn't some backup be reassuring? She'd convinced herself that Dorrance wouldn't come after her yet, but who knew how'd he react to what he'd see as today's debacle following his close call in Lieutenant Matson's backyard?

"Thank you," she forced herself to say, released the seat belt and opened the door. Then she made herself turn back to Boyd. "I'm sorry. I don't know why I even argued. I guess by this time you know I tend to get my back up when—" She hesitated, made momentarily uneasy by her inability to finish that sentence. She didn't like it when someone challenged her—but he hadn't done that.

The line of his mouth softened as he searched her face. "You don't like being scared."

Was that her problem? "No," she admitted, around a lump in her throat. Although, just because today she'd had a weird moment of seeing herself in Kristina didn't mean she was actually afraid. Only that she'd carried her empathy a little too far, given her profession. Cops had to retain some detachment, or they couldn't do their jobs.

Boyd said gruffly, "I wish you'd change your mind about—"

"Going on the run?" She made sure to sound bold. "Not a chance."

Before he could argue, she hopped out, slammed the door and walked to her own car. Her neck prickled with the knowledge that he hadn't taken his eyes off her. Just as she felt his stare drilling into the back of her head during the entire drive to her house.

SHE HADN'T BOUGHT the house until after the two of them quit seeing each other, so Boyd had never been inside, only seen it from the outside the one other time he'd followed her home. It was from Miguel that he'd heard she had decided she would rather live in her own place than with him at the ranch. At the time, he'd been tempted to look up the address and drive by—just curiosity—but wouldn't let himself. The word "stalker" had come to mind, particularly indefensible with him being a cop.

Turning into the driveway right behind her, he studied the single-story ranch-style house from a security standpoint. It reminded him of Guy Jonas's house, except worse, because it lacked a garage. If she'd been able to use a remote and drive right into an attached garage, he might even have honked and gone on his way.

No, he wouldn't. Dorrance had repeatedly demonstrated his skill at breaking into houses. Boyd wasn't going anywhere until they knew Melinda's was clear.

So he parked behind her and got out as she did the same. No eye rolls today. Echoing his movement, her hand went to the butt of her weapon and her head turned as she looked for trouble.

She waited for him to join her before taking the single step up to the small porch. "I was thinking," she said in a low voice. "We should send a unit by Dorrance's house. I'll bet he's gone by and knows it's empty."

"You're right." Boyd frowned. "Jonas's house, too. Hell, Cordova's is another possibility."

He watched their backs as she unlocked the door. Only as he heard the door opening did he start to turn back—just as she sucked in a breath.

She yanked the gun from its holster. He did the same without having to think. Then he saw what she had.

Her living room was trashed. Not ransacked the way a burglar might have done. *Destroyed* was the word that came to him. Mortar fire might have done this much damage.

She'd momentarily frozen just inside, her lips parted, eyes dilated in shock. He nudged her forward, then signaled toward the opening into a hall.

Melinda swallowed, visibly pulled herself together then nodded. She eased forward to flatten her back to the wall, ready to cover him as he started down the hall. A glance told him no one was in the kitchen, although it hadn't been spared. Food and broken dishes covered the floor. A back door had obviously been kicked open. Weapon held in readiness, she went into the first room on the left, a small bedroom converted to an office. When she backed out, he bumped open a door to see a bathroom, damaged but empty, then entered the last room, her bedroom. His nose had already told him some of what they'd find.

She let out a cry and brushed past him, coming to a stop a few feet from the bed. Her arms slowly sagged until her handgun pointed at the floor.

"This must have taken hours," she whispered.

"He *had* hours."

Bedding and mattress had been slashed. One closet door lay on the floor, where it had been stomped on, what had probably been a full-length mirror shattered into vicious, glittering pieces. The other closet door hung from one wheel on the track. Her clothes had been yanked out, slashed with a knife and then the intruder had urinated on them. Bureau and bedside table drawers all lay smashed on the floor, clothes in torn heaps. He'd slammed a lamp against the wall, opening a big hole in the plasterboard.

"Oh, God," Melinda whispered, her head turning. "He got his hands on *everything*."

Looking at her stricken face, he saw the moment

she cried out again. Holstering her gun, she raced to the vicinity of what had been her bureau, dropped to her knees and began frantically digging through the mess on the floor.

"It's the only picture I have! The only one! I have to find it."

Boyd joined her. "Your sister?"

"Yes!"

The sister who'd been murdered by one of their father's best friends. What she'd told Boyd had explained so much about her.

As he searched, too, he remembered the flickers of emotion she hadn't been able to hide, try as hard as she would.

Dad's buddy had been molesting Melinda's younger sister. Dad wouldn't believe it. Melinda had taken to guarding her sister like a pit bull, but Dad went so far as to insist Melinda go with him on what turned out to be a meaningless errand at a time Melinda had believed her sister was at a friend's. They returned to find the ten-year-old girl had been raped and strangled.

Good ole Dad? He reacted by sitting around getting drunk and crying and insisted Pete couldn't have done anything like that.

Since Pete had, he was arrested, tried and convicted. Refusing to stay with her sorry excuse for a father, Melinda had run away from home repeatedly until authorities placed her in foster care. Boyd knew she'd been able to take almost nothing from the house.

The sound that escaped from her throat now held pain he recognized. It was the noise parents always made when they found out a child was gone, or that their husband or wife had been taken from them by violence.

She held a twisted picture frame. Jagged shards of glass clung to the frame, and blood dripped from her hand. She hadn't even noticed. She was fumbling to gather shreds of paper.

Boyd gently took the frame from her and tossed it away, then wrapped her in his arms. "Melinda," he said roughly. "Sweetheart. You remember her. That's what's important."

He'd never seen her really cry, not like this. The sobs shook her slender body. For a minute, she seemed oblivious to his presence, but then she lifted a devastated gaze to his face.

"This was the only thing that mattered to me."

Hearing her despair wrenched something loose in him he doubted could ever be repaired. "It's *not* the only thing," he said insistently. "You know that. It was a photograph. You can still see your sister's face, can't you? Close your eyes and imagine it."

He dug deep to call up the sister's name. Elise. That was it.

She pressed her face to his chest. He was the one to close his eyes and lay his cheek against the top of her head. God, he couldn't stand seeing her so hurt. Maybe *this* was what had scared him as much as the idea of her being injured or killed. A woman so strong shouldn't sound so— No, damn it! Not broken. He had to believe nothing would break Melinda.

Fractured might be a better word. It didn't suggest a permanent state. Fractures could heal.

He was talking to her, with no idea what he'd been saying. Just…trying to give her comfort. He wanted to scoop her up and carry her out of this house, but what if Dorrance was outside watching? He'd love nothing more than seeing her face now.

No, that wasn't happening.

Melinda didn't cry as long as another woman might have. Any second, he expected her to retreat, physically and emotionally. To be embarrassed and even angry that she'd exposed her grief to him.

He wasn't going to let her get away with that.

Gently, he said, "Let me call Daniel."

"Daniel?" She lifted her face again, her eyes so swollen and red he wondered that she could see him. "What? Why…?"

"This is a crime scene now, and you're not going to be the one who has to process it." He hoped that didn't sound as grim as he felt.

After a moment, she bobbed her head.

He extracted his phone from his pocket and called Daniel, who answered immediately.

"I can tell you where Dorrance went after he found out he'd lost his hideaway," Boyd said. "He must have come straight to Melinda's place. He did his best to demolish it. As she said, he must have spent hours at it."

Daniel spat a couple of choice words. "You're with her?"

"Yes."

"You can stay put until I get there?"

"I won't leave her." Boyd met her eyes. "Just in case Dorrance is hanging around, we're staying inside."

"Then I'm on my way. I'll call the techs again—"

Boyd interrupted. "Let's seal the house and wait until morning to turn them loose in here. It's...worse than you're probably imagining."

Daniel agreed, and cut the connection. Boyd stowed his phone and said, "Let's get your face cleaned up."

Before Daniel or any other of her coworkers saw her. She wouldn't like that.

It took her a minute, but she nodded and let him help her up. Only then, as he steered her toward the doorway, did he see that one of her hands still formed a fist...one that enclosed scraps of the photograph that meant so much to her.

MELINDA SAT STIFFLY in the passenger seat of Boyd's SUV. She was going home with him, even though he'd never exactly asked her if she was okay with that. He just assumed. It was very Boyd-like. Maybe she should be ashamed to have been so compliant, but she couldn't yet work up even any indignation. She hadn't even thrown out an alternative.

She *wanted* to go home with Boyd. And maybe that wasn't smart, but she was doing it anyway.

Even if she'd hated the idea, she wasn't sure she could have summoned the least resistance. The anguish had ebbed, leaving in its place...nothing. *I'm numb*, she thought, except that wasn't quite true. Emotions swirled beneath the surface, a dangerous current. If she let herself think about— But she wouldn't. Tomorrow was soon enough.

What stunned her was discovering how *violated* she felt by the intrusion into her home, the destruction of her possessions. It shouldn't have come as any surprise; she'd seen the reaction over and over when she'd gone out on a report of a burglary. What had happened to her was worse; Dorrance hadn't only gotten into her house, touched things she owned, fingered her lingerie and peered into every private place, he'd then destroyed everything. Slashed and stomped and smashed. Urinated on her clothing in the worst insult of all.

He was making sure she knew he intended to do all those things to *her.*

She must have made a sound of some kind, because Boyd reached over and took her hand in his. He had such big hands, warm, strong and capable of such deftness, even delicacy.

He surely didn't assume she'd go to bed with him. Melinda almost shook her head. Of course he didn't. Whatever else she could say about him, he was too *decent*, too honorable, to take advantage of a woman in shock.

Funny, though, that he'd wanted her all along to stay with him at the ranch.

She focused enough to see that they were now on the ranch road, made of hard-packed dirt.

"Do you have a live-in girlfriend?" she asked, voice scratchy.

His head turned and his fingers tightened on hers. She didn't meet his eyes.

"No girlfriend."

She frowned, having a hard time imagining a man as beautiful as he was, as quintessentially male, ever not having a woman at his beck and call. But at least she wouldn't have to deal with that reality tonight.

"I'm assuming that if you were seeing anyone, you'd have called him instead of coming home with me."

Her couple of attempts to date since she and Boyd parted ways went nowhere. She thought maybe she'd given up. That's what happened when you thought you'd found the one person—

All she did was nod.

They passed the turnoff to his partner's cabin. She'd liked Gabe Decker even though he made her feel a little uncomfortable. It took her awhile to realize that Gabe's impassive face, his seeming stoicism, was his cover, just as Boyd's relaxed charm and confidence were his.

Boyd had been quite different in bed with her. Gabe probably was with his wife, too.

Wow, she was thinking about everything and anything *but* the monster who had to be stopped.

"Don't," Boyd said.

Startled, she looked at him. He couldn't possibly have read her mind.

"Your hand jerked." His voice lacked much inflection. "You started thinking about something that upset you. It can wait until tomorrow. You need a good night's sleep before you become a cop again."

"I'm always—"

"No, you aren't. And I should know."

Heat rose in her cheeks, despite her strange state of mind. He did know. He knew she was a woman, too—and he'd taken advantage of that because he didn't *want* her to be a cop at all. He couldn't possibly think—

"The task force meeting is soon enough." He came to a stop right in front of the massive log house he'd had built six years ago to replace what he'd told her was a shabby, traditional farmhouse with a cracked foundation. She'd never asked why he wanted such a big place, and he'd never volunteered the information. Why *hadn't* they had that discussion?

Because he'd expected her to reveal her sore places but hadn't been willing to do the same, Melinda suspected. She hadn't pushed, because she'd believed they would have time.

Maybe we do.

She didn't move even though he'd gotten out. All she did was watch him circle around to her side.

He hadn't given any indication he still felt the same way about her…but she knew that wasn't true. He was as intensely focused on her as he'd been back then, not trying to hide his tenderness or how protective he felt.

None of which answered the big question: whether he could accept the woman she'd made of herself after her father's betrayal and the loss of the only person she'd ever loved.

Except, maybe, Boyd.

Chapter Thirteen

"Ah. Lasagna." Boyd removed the labeled dish from his refrigerator. This being Friday, his housekeeper had left him a full casserole dish, intended to feed him for the next three days, needing only to be warmed up. "I hope you like it."

Melinda sat at the old farmhouse-style kitchen table, gazing straight ahead with dazed eyes. It took her a moment to focus on him.

"I love lasagna." She forced a smile. "Especially when it doesn't come out of the freezer case at the grocery store."

A picture flashed into his head of the food trampled on her kitchen floor. That probably included everything from her freezer.

He opened his mouth, about to tell her that his housekeeper was an excellent cook, but he stopped himself in time. She'd eaten Jennifer Langley's food several times. In fact, he'd first met Melinda when she came out to the ranch to interview the terrified little girl that Gabe and Trina had since adopted. They'd sat on the sofa in his living room, him leaning against a doorway trying to be unobtrusive. He'd had trouble taking his eyes off the slender, fine-boned female detective with the soft voice who'd been a natural at encouraging a scared kid to open up.

Frowning at the memory of his powerful reaction to Melinda McIntosh, he popped the dish in the microwave, the garlic bread in the convection oven, and decided not to bother with the broccoli. He didn't much like it anyway.

He poured two glasses of milk and carried them to the table, then set their places with napkins, silverware and plates. He was disturbed to see Melinda sitting so still. Outwardly she managed at the task force meetings, but he could always feel a sort of vibration coming from her. He suspected she was tapping a toe or toying with a rubber band or pen beneath the table. When they'd shared meals, she had been quick to jump to her feet and offer to help. Even sleeping, she was restless.

He gritted his teeth. He couldn't let himself remember how she'd felt curled up against him or squirming in search of a more comfortable position. They wouldn't be sleeping together tonight, no matter how much he wished it were so. *She'd* sleep better in his arms, and he'd prefer having her so close, he didn't have to lie staring at the dark ceiling worrying about her.

Right now, she was dull, her personality in hiding. He hoped that's all it was. She was taking the destruction of her home worse than she would have a physical attack on *her*. Everyone needed a sanctuary, and hers was gone. Plus... Boyd suspected the loss of that single, precious photograph was the worst part. He couldn't forget her thin cry, or the way she'd all but screamed, *This was the only thing that mattered to me!*

In a way, her sister had been killed again today.

After the appliances beeped, he carried their dinner to the table and then, when she still didn't move, dished up for both of them.

Melinda stared down at her serving of lasagna. Once again, he sensed it took her some effort to say anything. "It smells good, but... I'm not that hungry."

"Did you have lunch?" He knew the answer; their day had been too eventful for either of them to take a meal break.

She lifted her head and blinked a few times. Her forehead crinkled. "I guess not."

"Then eat even if you don't feel like it. Come morning, you need to be strong."

A beat slower than would have been natural, she nodded. Satisfied to see the first bite go in her mouth, Boyd started eating himself. And, damn, he was starved. His big body required a lot more fuel than did her much more slender one.

She paused after a few bites to tear the slice of garlic bread in half, then quarters. Was she going to shred it so that he wouldn't notice she hadn't eaten any of it? But she lifted one piece and took a bite out of it.

She surprised him by asking, "Is Mrs. Langley still with you?"

He liked that she was curious, and glad to talk if that would distract her.

"She is. She claims I'm the perfect employer. I'll eat just about anything she prepares, I'm reasonably tidy and I'm hardly ever underfoot."

Melinda surprised him by chuckling. Maybe good food had been just what she needed. "She's got a point."

"She's a proud mama right now," he added. "The youngest of her two kids just graduated with honors from Pomona University."

"That's in southern California, right?"

"Yep. Top-tier liberal arts school. Her daughter picked it because she was desperate—or so she said—to live someplace that was actually populated with two-legged mammals instead of four. She wanted museums, restaurants, concerts. Since she's been accepted to Columbia University for law school, I don't think she plans any immediate return to ranching country."

Melinda laughed but then said, "That's sad for Mrs. Langley."

"From what I gather, you couldn't pay her enough to live in an apartment in Portland, never mind New York City. I think she'll be happy with visits from her kids. They seem to talk often."

He turned his attention back to eating, as Melinda did the same, albeit slower. She suddenly laid down her fork, though.

"You said you'll eat 'just about' anything. What won't you eat?"

He raised his eyebrows. "Oysters. Cooked spinach. Brussels sprouts. I'm not all that fond of broccoli, either, which is why we're not having a vegetable with dinner."

"But if Mrs. Langley had cooked and served it, you'd have eaten it."

"Yeah."

"I had no idea you'd let anyone persuade you to do a single thing you didn't want to," Melinda said thoughtfully.

Good to know she thought of him as an autocrat.

"I'm capable of bowing to common sense," he countered. "Broccoli is good for me. Taste isn't the point." Was this the right or wrong time to talk about them? He couldn't decide, but did say, "I can change, you know. It...just doesn't come easily to me."

Her startled gaze met his. Neither of them so much as blinked for a good minute. She clearly knew he wasn't talking about his tastes in food.

She nibbled on her lower lip, distracting him from her haunting eyes. "I've...wondered. If I hadn't just walked out."

"I knew better than to make a demand like that." He had to press the heel of his hand against his breastbone to quell the sharp pain under it. "But..." He gusted out a breath. "You scared me. And I'd made a vow."

"What was that vow?" Melinda barely spoke above a whisper.

"That I'd never again let myself love a woman whose job put her into regular danger."

She shrugged, as if what he'd said didn't matter. "And there I was."

"Yeah." He had to clear his throat. "There you were." She'd come as a shocker to him, no question.

Boyd couldn't just keep eating, downplay how important this conversation was. He could only wait for her to make the next move…if she gave a damn why he'd made a vow that ruled her out.

Melinda tore apart more of her bread, reminding him unpleasantly of the scraps of that photograph.

The only thing that mattered to her. Mattered so much, he'd asked one of the techs to gather those scraps so he could try to have the photo restored.

Now, when he'd almost given up, she said, "You lost someone."

Did her asking mean *he* mattered, too?

"Yeah." Funny, how he had to work to summon a picture of Raquel's face. Passing years did that. But it came. Melinda didn't look anything like Raquel, except for the thick dark hair. Well, similar height, too, and both were athletic women. Fighters, in different ways. "She was a soldier. Part of a unit that guarded supply convoys. I worried, but she spent most of her time on the base. Afghanistan," he added. "She worried about me. It wasn't supposed to be the other way around."

Melinda watched him, expression solemn.

"Her family was traditional. Her grandparents came to the US from Costa Rica. They weren't happy about her joining the army. She was supposed to work in the family business, a growing chain of restaurants in Houston. Get married, have babies. She wanted to see the world, have some adventures." He had a feeling his smile was a failure. "I don't suppose they'd have been any happier about me."

"You wanted to marry her?"

"We'd just started talking about it." He shrugged. "She resisted. I wasn't anywhere near ready to retire from the military, and Raquel had no intention of getting stuck back home, alone in officer housing while I was gone for months at a time."

Man, he thought, who was he kidding? Melinda and Raquel would have understood each other at first sight.

"What happened?"

"IED. She was in the lead vehicle. It went off right beneath her. They couldn't really even come up with a body to bury."

"Oh, Boyd." Melinda stood so suddenly, her chair rocked. She came around the table and put her arms around him.

He buried his face between her breasts and held on. Mostly, Raquel had been a dream, one that had faded in the intervening years, but talking about her brought the memory of pain.

"I'm so sorry," Melinda murmured, her cheek against his head. "Did you have leave? A chance to go home and, I don't know, talk to her family?"

"No. We were in the middle of an operation. It was almost a week after her death before I even heard about it. I…had to go on."

"Push everything you felt out of sight."

He gave a rough laugh and straightened, letting his arms fall away. Reluctantly, but pity wasn't what he wanted from this woman. "Yeah. I'm here to say that doesn't work so well."

Melinda backed away in recognition of his withdrawal, and after a moment returned to her place at the table, although he doubted she'd eat any more. He'd kind of lost his appetite, too.

"How long ago was this?" she asked.

"Ah…" There was a time, he could have told her to the day. Now, he had to think back. "Seven years ago. You'd have been dealing with Dorrance right around then."

Their eyes met again.

"I should have known there was something like that."

He shoved away his plate. "How about some apple pie?"

"That…actually sounds good. Thank you."

This time, she insisted on clearing the table, rinsing their plates and loading them in the dishwasher while he served the pie, including ice cream for himself. Then they sat back down.

The silence while they ate was peaceful on the surface, but he knew a lot simmered beneath it. He was proved right when she said, "So, if I'd argued back when we split up, would you have backed down?"

Boyd had to be honest. "I don't know. I'd like to think we could have…compromised, but that was never possible, was it?"

"What'd you think, I'd switch to working dispatch? Something like that?"

"Maybe."

"And what were *you* going to give?" she asked, the razor edge not so well hidden in her voice.

"Nothing as meaningful," he had to admit. "I was stunned when you just said, 'Forget about it,' and left."

"You could have called me later. Come after me."

He realized he was glaring at her. "I thought *you'd* be back, calling me a jerk. When I never heard from you—" A chasm had opened at his feet, that's what. All he'd been able to think was, he'd let himself fall for another woman who chose her job over him.

And he'd been too damn scared to accept that, with both Raquel and Melinda, the job had been part of the woman, and therefore a good part of why he'd fallen for each of them.

"So you didn't change your mind," she said now, flatly.

"At the time, no."

She'd heard what he was saying, all right, because skittishness showed. "I can't deal with this right now."

He could do nothing but nod. Had he really been deluding himself that she'd throw herself into his arms and he could carry her up to his bed? After she'd seen a recurrence of one of her worst nightmares today?

Idiot.

"Okay," he said. "What are you thinking for tomorrow?"

The relief on her face at the change of subject shamed him.

"I want to talk to Kristina Morgan. I hope she'll be in good enough shape to tell us what she learned about Dorrance."

"I can't imagine anything she heard will help find him, but I'd sure as hell like to know how he homed in on her."

Melinda nodded. "I would, too. You don't mind driving me to the hospital in the morning?"

An officer at the scene this evening had driven her Subaru to the police station and parked in back. Leaving it in front of her demolished house hadn't seemed like a good idea.

Boyd scowled at her. "Of course not. I'd like to sit in when you talk to Kristina—" Seeing Melinda about ready to fire up, he raised a hand. "I won't even try. She'll be more comfortable talking to a woman, but I'll wait for you. Daniel can hold off the morning meeting until we get to the station."

"Okay." She suddenly looked shy. "Would you mind if I took a shower and went to bed? I'm really beat."

"Of course not." He pushed back his chair and rose. "Come on. I'll find you something you can sleep in, and I can wash what you're wearing, if you want."

"That would be good." Melinda offered him a twisted smile. "I suppose I'd better find time to shop tomorrow, too."

"I'm afraid so," he said gently.

"I need to tackle that mess."

"My advice?" At her nod, he said, "Get a dumpster out there, then hire someone. They can toss everything too damaged for use, set the intact stuff aside for you to go through. A stranger won't take the same emotional hit you would picking up every single item." Seeing the emotions shimmering in her eyes made it hard to go on, but this needed to be said. "You'll need to get repairs done, too, before the house is livable again."

"That's true. I don't know if it will ever feel like home again," she said softly. "Funny, I'd just had that thought about Kristina. I mean, whether she'd be able to live in her house again."

The only, and probably useless thing he could think to say was, "Give it time."

Melinda offered him a shaky smile. "Thank you. For everything. I mean, today."

"You're welcome." Seeing her startled expression, he realized that had sounded curt. He didn't want her thanks. He wanted—

There he went again, wanting to push. Which, he acknowledged ruefully, was his nature.

"Let me show you where you'll sleep," he said, and led the way toward the wide staircase formed of slabs of pine.

He gestured her into a guest bedroom, but she came to a stop in the doorway, looking at him. She dampened her lips with her tongue, betraying some nerves. Boyd couldn't help himself. He lifted his hand and stroked her cheek, ending with his thumb pressing lightly on that tempting mouth. Melinda trembled, he couldn't mistake that, and her eyes darkened. She might have even swayed toward him.

He thought he'd started to bend his head when she jerked and took a big step back, panic awakened.

He clenched his teeth, growled, "Just a second," and fetched a T-shirt and a pair of sweatpants with a drawstring waist from his room. Wordlessly, he handed them over, waited until she passed him her dirty clothes through a three-inch crack between door and frame, and took them downstairs with him. Then he pretty well paced until the washer finished and he could throw everything into the dryer.

She'd been naked, just on the other side of that door.

He wouldn't be sleeping like a baby tonight.

WITH THE COLORS of the bruises on her face turning garish, Kristina almost looked worse the next morning. Her responses came slowly, as if she had to work at grasping the questions. But when Melinda had asked in the first place if she was able to talk, she'd immediately said, "Yes. I…don't know if I can help, but if there's anything…"

True to her word, Sherry Williams had been in the chair by Kristina's bedside when Melinda arrived, a fierce guardian. She'd gone down to the cafeteria to get some breakfast and coffee, having apparently spent the night.

Melinda left the door half open, aware Boyd leaned against the wall in the corridor eavesdropping.

Working their painful way through Dorrance's arrival at the house and the initial brutality took more out of Kristina than Melinda liked, but it had to be done.

Kristina kneaded the bedclothes with arthritic hands. "It was my fault he knew about me," she said in a low voice. "I was…such a fool."

"*Nothing* about this was your fault," Melinda said sternly.

"Oh." The older woman focused on Melinda's face. "You're right. I didn't mean it that way. Only that I got to know him years ago, when I was a nurse here at the hospital. He was severely injured when a lift failed at the garage where he worked. I covered his floor, night shift, and he had to stay for, oh, almost a week, I think." Her mouth twisted into an almost-smile. "Things get slow in the middle of the night. He wasn't sleeping well. We…started talking. It seemed to me that he was lonely, too. There was nothing romantic." The wrinkles on her forehead deepened. "Just…us sharing some of the dark hours. So, you see, he knew I lived alone in a too-big house on acreage. I told him I had no intention of moving, that it was home even if downsizing would have been smarter for me."

As it turned out, Melinda couldn't help thinking, it would have been way smarter.

She shuddered. "I was horrified when he was arrested back then, and I learned what he was really like." She made a sound in her throat. "After he, um, forced himself into my house, he told me he'd looked me up back then. Even driven by the house a few times. Decided I wasn't worth his while. He made a point of saying I still wasn't, saggy old woman I am, but he'd had to *settle*."

Melinda huffed out a breath. "I don't think he has a single redeeming feature. There are men on death row who hold on to their humanity. I'm not sure Gene Dorrance ever had any."

"No," Kristina whispered.

They talked for a while longer. Melinda asked if he'd implied he would let Kristina go.

Her head moved slightly against the pillow in a shake. "He said I'd be glad when he was through with me. 'I like to bury my girlfriends.'" She shuddered. "He actually said that. *Girlfriends*."

Melinda leaned forward. "I've always suspected he'd held other women captive and killed them, but we couldn't prove it. We never had a clue where he might have buried them."

Kristina plucked some more at the bedclothes, her hands shaky. "He didn't say, except... There was something about a grove. He came back one night, enraged—" Her throat worked. "He—" After a moment, she murmured, "You know what he did to me. He said...he said he might just dump me there, instead of burying me, because the cops had ruined it for him."

A grove. One the cops had ruined for him.

It was all Melinda could do to keep from leaping to her feet. No wonder Dorrance knew that clump of quaking aspen trees so well.

Dear Lord, if they could find the graves...

Had Boyd heard? Would he already be making calls? This was the first real clue...but after so many years, the soil would have settled, vegetation regrown.

And Dorrance would still be out there, angrier than ever at her.

Chapter Fourteen

By the time she came out of the hospital room, Boyd had already contacted Daniel, who called for a handler to bring a cadaver dog to the bridge on the south side of the aspen grove.

"Apparently she's in the middle of a training session," he told Melinda. "Her name's Sarah Sutton. She has several dogs she uses for volunteer work. Mostly search and rescue, I guess, but she's trained one to sniff out accelerants in suspicion fires, and has a Lab with a gift for finding bodies."

"I've worked with her," Melinda said, as he drove out of the parking lot, "but I thought she did only search and rescue. Did Daniel tell her how long ago those bodies would have been buried?"

"I'm sure he did. He wouldn't waste her time if she and her dog couldn't help."

"No. God, I hope we can find the graves! At least the women's parents would *know*."

"Yeah," he said in the gruff way that felt like a gentle touch with calloused fingers.

Her cheek tingled with the memory of yesterday

evening's touch, and she wished she hadn't been a coward.

He didn't seem to notice her reaction, continuing, "I just wish we had a hint where Dorrance might have gone to earth."

"Bad pun," she pointed out.

He gave a grunt that was almost a laugh.

Melinda kept sneaking glances at him during the short drive to the police station. She'd shocked herself last night by dropping off to sleep practically the minute she slipped between the sheets, and not waking until Boyd had rapped on her door this morning.

Because I felt safe.

Something she would usually hate to admit. She kept *herself* safe. She'd never been willing to depend on anyone else for something so basic, not since she'd failed to protect Elise.

What surprised her was realizing that she didn't mind knowing that she'd been leaning on Boyd as much as she should. For all their history, he hadn't said anything to make her think he felt that because he was bigger and stronger, it meant he was also superior. He'd even hinted that he knew he was wrong to ask her to give up her job so that he didn't have to worry about her.

At least she understood now. At the time, she hadn't so much as wondered whether he had something in his past that hurt as much as her sister's murder had hurt her. It said something about her that she *hadn't* wondered.

She wrinkled her nose, remembering the way he'd

thrown out his demand, completely confident she'd jump to diminish herself because he'd made his pronouncement. And *that* said something about *him*.

Of course, his years as an army officer had given him more practice in throwing out orders and assuming anyone within earshot would jump to meet them than could possibly be healthy for anyone.

"Did I miss anything?" he asked now, after a fleeting, hard to read glance.

"You mean after she talked about the graves? I don't think so." She was quiet for a minute, before exclaiming, "Where *is* he?"

"I wish I knew." That grim tone matched her mood. "I have the helicopter back up in the air, and we have an all points bulletin out on the Camry now that we know the model and color. Switching license plates won't help him."

"No."

"He lost his backup vehicle, too."

That must have made him almost as mad as losing his hostage had.

She focused as Boyd turned just past the police station into the parking lot. It seemed to her that the media presence was diminishing. In one way, she hated the pressure they brought to bear, but what if people were tired of constant tension and had decided to shrug off the worry? After all, there were other stories to follow on the local news.

Actually, she wasn't sure whether that was true or not. *Her* attention had been single-minded for…

she had to count. A week now. No, eight days. Nine? She'd lost track.

"Task force meeting," she mumbled.

That earned her another glance from Boyd as he parked. "We have information to share the others probably haven't all heard. Maybe someone else does, too. Or will have an idea worth pursuing."

"Sure." Dispirited, she got out of the SUV and waited for him before heading into the building.

Unfortunately, no one else around the table in the conference room had any meaningful news or even ideas. Daniel's update on Lieutenant Matson was positive, though; doctors had decided when to release him from the hospital.

Daniel finished his report with a grimace. "Which means putting him and his wife into hiding."

There was a moment of depressed silence.

The FBI agent said thoughtfully, "This guy has a gift for passing under the radar."

"He probably always has," Boyd commented. "And yeah, he's had a way of making people uncomfortable, but not always. Kristina Morgan sounds as if she liked him. Felt as if they had a lot in common. Really, the guy lived in Sadler for a lot of years without drawing much attention at all. None from law enforcement, until Andrea Kudelka somehow briefly overpowered him."

"That's true," Daniel agreed. "Not sure where to go with that, though." When no one else commented, he said, "Detective Yates, have you learned anything about the pickup truck that was in the Morgan woman's garage?"

"It's a 1998 Chevy, black and rusting," the young detective said. "I haven't looked up the VIN number, but finding out where he got it doesn't seem very pressing now. If he purchased it, the seller hasn't turned in the required title change. Given the number of pickup trucks on the road locally, this one would have been good camouflage, but it doesn't want to start and spits out clouds of black exhaust. Joe Bailey—" the mechanic who took care of the department's fleet "—says Dorrance was damn lucky to make it across the state in that derelict. It has a hundred and seventy-three thousand miles on it," he added.

So Dorrance had needed not only a hostage and a bolt-hole, but also new transportation—all provided for him by Kristina Morgan. All stolen from him yesterday.

"No sightings of the Camry?" he asked, knowing the answer. Someone would have said.

Daniel shook his head, and Aaron Loftis, the CAU rep said, "Calls to the tip line are down. Might be time for another press conference."

Although Melinda suspected that Chief Austin loved nothing more than standing behind the microphone, the center of attention, even he must be losing enthusiasm. The questions weren't nearly as sympathetic as they'd been, for one thing. And he'd be able to do nothing but flash Dorrance's photo—again—and say—again, "We need the public's help to locate our suspect," and declare that this cop killer was likely driving a gray Toyota Camry.

From what Melinda could gather, Kristina's identity hadn't been breached yet, and they wanted to keep it that way. The press wouldn't like being told a victim had been rescued, sending Dorrance on the run again, without the addition of any details.

The group briefly discussed the trashing of Melinda's house, then she detailed the interview with Kristina and the hope that a cadaver dog might be able to locate the grave or graves Melinda had always believed were out there somewhere.

Loftis frowned. "Who is this woman? She's not on my list of resources."

Daniel assured him that she'd assisted several law enforcement agencies in Oregon and northern California, after which Loftis decided to join those at the possible gravesites.

As the meeting broke up, Daniel stopped Boyd and Melinda, letting them know he'd just gotten a text from the dog handler, who planned to meet them forty-five minutes from now. He handed over Melinda's car keys, too.

"You probably saw it parked out back."

She nodded, although she hadn't even looked.

He joined Loftis and the two men departed, talking as they went about the challenges of locating old graves without a fairly precise starting point.

She ought to be worrying about the same thing, but instead had the passing thought that she should stop at her desk, check email and see how high the stack of paperwork on her desk had grown. Somehow, she couldn't work up any interest. Except—oh, God, she was so behind on the reports *she'd* have to write.

Boyd, of course, hadn't gone anywhere without her. Even aside from his physical presence, it was impossible to forget he was there given that those eyes rested on her no matter what else she was doing, or who she was talking to.

Straightening away from the wall in the now empty hallway outside the conference room, Boyd asked, "Any reason we should drive separately out to the aspen grove?"

At least he hadn't questioned her right to be there. Boyd's presence was a given with the site well outside the city limits and therefore in his jurisdiction.

Did she want to drive herself?

When she hesitated, his expression darkened.

That stiffened her spine. "You'd rather I give up even that vestige of my independence?"

His dark eyebrows arched. "That's what you think of me?"

After a moment, she felt her shoulders sag. "No. I'm sorry. I appreciate everything you've done, especially given our past and my, well, attitude. I… hope you won't mind me staying with you for a few more days, until I can figure something else out."

He studied her for a moment, then said calmly, "No hurry. In fact, as far as I'm concerned, you don't need to figure anything out." He smiled slightly. "I have in mind you staying for good."

Melinda's mouth dropped open, but after his bombshell he walked away, heading for the exit sign at the end of the hall. She was left gaping at his broad back, torn between astonishment and aggravation that he'd just throw something like that out, and a thrill she couldn't deny. She had absolutely no idea how to respond to what he'd said.

Then her eyes narrowed. She'd trot after him, as he assumed she would—but that didn't mean she couldn't stroll right past him and drive herself after all.

Take that, she thought with satisfaction she knew full well was darn right childish.

FULLY AWARE THAT it was his fault he had to watch her in the rearview mirror instead of having her sitting beside him within touching distance while they squabbled and maybe even came to some kind of understanding about their future, Boyd gave himself an ass-kicking as he drove. What the hell had he been thinking?

He wasn't, that's what. The truth had just fallen out of his mouth without any thought, and he couldn't remember the last time that happened. It was particularly foolish where Melinda was concerned. He knew how sensitive she was, and why, and then what did he do but confirm her belief he was a dictatorial jackass?

Maybe because he was?

He switched his gaze from the road ahead to

scowl at the sight of her red Subaru, hanging farther back than he liked.

But then one corner of his mouth quirked. No, he hadn't enjoyed her cool, challenging gaze as she sauntered by him, hitting the "unlock" button on her remote, but now that he thought about it, he *had* appreciated the saunter. Her hips had swung that extra little bit to send him a message.

Oh, yeah—she'd still be going home with him tonight. *After* she put him in his place. He grinned.

Nearing Cordova's place, all amusement and anticipation left him. He couldn't help thinking about how close Kristina had come to being murdered, her body tossed out by the side of the road. And then there was their grim purpose this morning.

Boyd slowed down and started watching for the unmarked turn to the left. There it was. His tires crunched on gravel and spit out dust in a plume to envelop first Melinda's Subaru, then Daniel's department-issue SUV.

He slowed even more when he got to the timber-built bridge, but it felt sturdy when he rolled onto it. If there really were ranches out here, the bridge had presumably been designed to support stock trailers.

Not far on the other side of it, a dusty blue pickup was pulled off onto the shoulder. Someone sat inside, and he felt sure that was a dog in the passenger seat. He tucked in behind and parked.

Melinda and Daniel followed suit. Boyd left greetings to Daniel, who'd made the contact with the dog handler, and instead surveyed the dirt verge of the road.

Even as seldom used as this road seemed to be, would Dorrance want to carry a body from his car down a slight incline toward the creek? All it would take was suddenly finding himself speared by the twin beams of headlights.

Instinct said no. Boyd crossed the road to walk along that side. Maybe they'd taken the reference to "the grove" too literally, but the drop-off was more pronounced here, the land too open. He ignored the cluster of two men and two women still conferring when he recrossed the road and kept walking. If there was a way to get down closer to the cluster of aspens, Dorrance hadn't used it the night he'd set up the ambush here, but that made sense. He'd have planned for a quick getaway if events went bad, as they had.

Boyd turned at the soft fall of footsteps behind him. Melinda, of course.

"What are you thinking?" she asked.

He told her.

She nodded. "The only thing is, he probably didn't bury more than a couple of bodies out here. At least, we have only two missing women from that period. Also…" She hesitated.

"It's been nine years plus," he conceded. "If it were only tracks he'd made, they'd be gone. But what I was thinking is that this would be a good place to bring the kids to wade and picnic, or skinny-dip, or throw in a fishing line. If somebody stumbled on an easy route to drive close to the creek, others would find it, too."

"You're right. What if the turnoff is farther up

the road? With this scruffy growth, we might not
be able to see it."

Back by the cars, the woman, lean and athletic,
had clipped a leash on the dog, a big yellow Labrador, and was sliding down toward the creek. Loftis
and Daniel followed her.

Boyd nodded toward them. "Why don't you go
ahead? I might drive a little farther to check it out."

"I'll come with you," she said firmly. "If there's
a place he could have parked down there, that would
narrow down how much ground we have to cover."

They walked back to his vehicle. Daniel glanced
over his shoulder, but didn't demand an explanation
for why they were climbing in and about to drive
away.

Melinda sat tensely beside Boyd as he edged out
of the line of parked cars, but kept her mouth shut.
Apparently she shared his feeling that this wasn't a
time or place for anything that didn't have to do with
their purpose here.

The land in this area did some gentle rolling. He
saw what might be the crumbling remnants of a ba-
salt formation. The road dropped past it, and damn,
there was a track, well-used although clearly not of-
ficially maintained, leading back toward the creek.
Seeing the same thing he did, Melinda stiffened.

He turned carefully onto it. Not maintained by
anybody, it had ruts that made the SUV lurch and
his head connect with the roof a couple of times, but
led straight through sagebrush and junipers to the

creek. The turn-around there would give space for three or four cars to park.

It placed them a good half mile upstream from where the handler was set to start her dog to work.

Boyd pulled out his cell phone and called Daniel.

TWO HOURS LATER, the dog alerted. The handler praised him and Daniel hammered the kind of flag surveyors used into the ground. They were right at the edge of the grove, but far enough outside it that someone digging wouldn't have had to contend with roots, yet the soil might retain some softening moistness from the creek.

Boyd looked around for any natural markers. Would Dorrance have been able to find this exact spot again?

Close enough, apparently, because ten minutes later, the Labrador alerted again, and they marked yet another spot.

Daniel was on the phone again, calling for help and tools to dig. At this point, the rest of them just watched as the dog searched an increasingly widening grid.

Somehow, it wasn't a shock when the dog found two more places worthy of exploration. After rewarding her dog each time, the handler kept it up for another couple of hours while the CSI team and a couple of off-duty officers joined the rest of them and they started to dig at the first two sites.

The day was hot. Boyd was glad to be wearing flexible tactical boots instead of the polished cowboy boots he wore when he expected to be on camera. During his shifts digging, he had to stop frequently to wipe sweat out of his eyes. He wasn't alone. He'd shed his uniform shirt within minutes but kept on the white T-shirt he'd worn beneath. Between copious sweat and dirt, he could tell it was destined for the ragbag.

Melinda and the two CSI techs present paced between the growing holes. Melinda had wanted to help, but to her obvious annoyance, none of the men gave way.

Boyd's hole was a couple of feet down when his shovel scraped on something. Not for the first time—they'd hit rocks early on, plentiful enough he'd wondered if the gravedigger had piled them on before covering them with dirt.

But, as he had every other time, he stopped and crouched, using his hand to brush away reddish soil to reveal a stained oval object with a couple of cracks. He knew what he'd found.

He stood and called for a tech. "I've got something."

A couple of men kept digging, but everyone else present gathered around the hole and watched as she used a brush to gently expose more of what they all knew was a skull.

Boyd switched his gaze to Melinda, who stood with her arms crossed on the other side of the hole—the grave—and stared unblinking at the evidence of what she'd always insisted she knew: that Gene Dorrance had held and murdered women before the rescue of Andrea Kudelka and Erica Warner.

Her expression was so closed, he hated to think what bubbled beneath the lid she'd jammed tight.

Chapter Fifteen

Melinda had been conscious all day of Boyd's occasional, searching gaze. Because of it—because she didn't dare let him weaken her—she'd kept her distance from him, although she, in turn, couldn't help watching him hard at work, too.

He seemed indefatigable. Sweat plastered the thin fabric of his T-shirt to hard muscle, making him look less civilized than he did in his usual crisp white shirt with pearl snaps, dark trousers and dark suit coat. His hair was wet and disheveled from all the times he ran his fingers through it—and from the once he walked away from a grave to crouch by the creek and splash water over his head and shoulders.

Not until they started toward their cars did he and she have a moment to talk.

"From the minute we got there, you knew Dorrance must have had a way to drive down closer to the creek." The question had nagged at her all day.

Boyd flicked a glance her way. "Made sense."

"I wouldn't have thought of it." She usually kept her awareness of her own shortcomings to herself, but she owed him one. "We'd have wasted hours, maybe even given up."

"Maybe, maybe not. Daniel would have had the same thought once he had a minute to look around."

"Because of your military experience."

"Thinking about routes and tracking is part of it."

She unlocked her door, tired but needing to say this. "I should grovel. I remember what I said back then." Still hurting, she'd lashed out after he was elected sheriff and they'd been forced to work together on the hunt for the serial killer. She couldn't remember the exact words, but she'd been so sure his years in the military didn't give him the qualifications to be sheriff, whatever the voters thought.

A crease in his cheek let her know he was smiling. "But you were right, too. I didn't know anything about criminal investigation."

After a moment, she nodded. Maybe he hadn't, but he had learned. He'd been…more of a partner this past week than she could ever remember having before. Using his head, offering a strong wall at her back.

The knowledge was humbling, and she knew then that she couldn't have been more wrong about him.

It was a shock to realize she trusted him more than anybody but Daniel, and their relationship was primarily a working one. Off the job, they were friends in a casual way because of her friendship with his wife, Lindsay.

Melinda felt a whole lot for Boyd that was light-years past "friend."

As she followed him home to the ranch, she wished she was beside him instead of still maintaining that distance. Her determination to assert her independence this morning felt petty.

He turned off the highway, her right behind, the tires changing sound on the packed dirt and gravel ranch road. She felt weird—almost as if she were having an out-of-body experience—during the half mile drive to his log house. He must have used a remote, because a wide door rolled up on an outbuilding she wouldn't have identified as a garage, revealing two open spaces inside. He parked, and she followed. Having their vehicles out of sight and locked in was smart, she had to admit.

When she got out, Boyd was waiting. The door glided down behind them and he held out a hand, before glancing down at it with distaste and pulling it back.

She didn't care how dirty his hand was. She snatched it up and squeezed hard. For a moment, he only looked down at her, but then his clasp tightened and he led her to the wide front steps to the porch, up and inside.

Boyd stopped, flicking on a light, his intent gaze on her. "You were right about that SOB."

It was the first time they'd talked about it.

"I wish I hadn't been." She'd been haunted by the ghosts of the dead women, but now the graves would take their place.

"I know," he said gruffly. He seemed to be waiting

for something more, but finally he released her hand. "I need a shower before we think about dinner."

She hadn't worked hard the way he had, but she'd sweated plenty just standing out in the hot sun for so much of the day. Since she hadn't managed to shop for clothes, though, she'd either be putting the same dirty clothes back on, or Boyd's way-too-big sweats and T-shirt. Or she could wait until bedtime.

"I'll check out your refrigerator," she suggested, backing away. "You go ahead."

"I left a note this morning asking Jennifer to run into town and pick up some basics for you." His smile was so faint, Melinda might have missed it. "Somehow, I suspected you'd be too busy to do anything about it yourself."

"Clothes, you mean? Oh. That was really nice of you. And of her. I'd like a shower, too. I have to admit. I feel like—" She made herself stop.

"You want to wash his contamination off you?"

"Something like that."

"Then come on." He held out that big, filthy hand again. Knuckles were scraped, she saw, and his fingernails were broken and dirty, too, but his strength was just what she needed right now.

They climbed the stairs side by side, as if they'd done so a hundred times instead of the few occasions she'd been with him in this house.

"I had an idea," she heard herself say. Better to concentrate on catching Dorrance than on the fact that the ground had shifted between her and Boyd.

That they were alone in his house, possibilities she had given up on open once more.

He looked sharply at her and came to a stop in the hall outside the guest room.

"We've let him take the offensive. You notice he hasn't emailed me in days."

"I've noticed." There was enough grit in the two words to scrape more skin from his body. "I'm surprised he hasn't sent a picture taken at your house."

She was, too, but maybe he didn't consider the destruction to be a victory.

"I snapped a couple of pictures today."

Boyd's eyebrows rose, and for good reason. Cops didn't take their own photos at crime scenes. Otherwise, they were setting themselves up for their phones to become part of the court record.

"Not of the graves or anything. Of you and Daniel opening the back of the hearse. A few like that."

They hadn't really needed a vehicle as big as the hearse, given that all they found in those graves was bones, lacking substance to fill out body bags, although they'd used those anyway to make sure every tiny bone and piece of dirt—or other evidence— made it back to the lab. Techs, including a contingent from CAU, had used brushes to clear the skeletons and, after endless photographs taken in situ, been careful to remove them and lay them out again just as they'd been in the graves. The body bags were supported by stretchers so that nothing could shift during transportation.

"You're thinking of sending him a photo so he knows we found the graves."

"I'm betting that will shake him up." She wanted to do a lot more than that, but had to take what she could get. "The more we can rattle him, the more likely he is to screw up."

"You need to clear it with Daniel."

"He's heading SPD's investigation, but you're running the county's."

His eyebrows twitched. "As you've pointed out in the past, I don't have the background and experience he does. Or you, for that matter."

Melinda made a face at him.

Boyd smiled, bent forward and kissed her lightly on the lips. "Why don't you shower, then give him a call?"

"Okay." She smiled weakly and let herself into the guest room.

BOYD BENT HIS HEAD forward, savoring the powerful beat of water on his neck and back, but the simple pleasure didn't reduce his tension. Fear for Melinda collided with this powerful resurgence of feelings for her. Did she want him as much as he wanted her? Was she ready to relent and come to bed with him tonight?

The chemistry was still there, he knew it was. Knew she felt it, too. But for the first time in his life, that wasn't enough. Yeah, he'd felt more than physical desire for Raquel, but their relationship had developed naturally, without a lot of agonizing until near the end, when they butted up against where they'd take it. And Melinda—he'd been in love with her the first time around, he just hadn't known how much. Hadn't analyzed why she hit him so hard from the first meeting.

Thus his stupid demand.

With a groan, he tipped his head back so that the hot water ran over his face.

His instinct was to push it with Melinda tonight. Those aggressive instincts were part of him, meaning that patience came hard for him. Even so…he knew he couldn't do that to her. He couldn't forget what Dorrance's assault on Melinda—and that's what it had been, for all that she hadn't been physically present—had taken out of her. Today, he'd seen grief to go along with the satisfaction at finding answers, and he'd heard humility when she apologized for the things she'd said to him, even though he'd known he deserved every word at the time.

The last thing she needed was to have him come on to her like a charging bull.

He mumbled some profanities, got a mouthful of water he had to spit out and turned off the faucet.

The hall bathroom door was closed when he passed it after getting mostly dressed. He had to grit his teeth at the images that filled his head: Melinda's long, slender body, her high, firm breasts, legs that went on forever. Was she toweling off right now? Had she run the water as hot as he had, making her ivory skin pink?

He swore again and made himself keep going,

even when he heard the quiet sound of that door opening behind him.

Some evenings he'd find the makings for a dinner he had to cook himself—say, steaks for the grill, or the already sliced and diced ingredients for a stir-fry. But Jennifer would have observed the long hours he was working, and obviously knew he had a guest, so tonight's meal was one of her casseroles, easy to reheat, along with homemade sourdough rolls and a salad ready to put on the table.

He set the casserole to warming while he listened to Melinda talking on the phone behind him. When he did turn, he saw that she was staring at his bare feet, a blush chasing across her face. His feet weren't particularly sexy—but he thought hers were. She was definitely reacting to something.

Pay attention to what you're doing.

He waited until they'd sat down to eat before he asked what Daniel thought.

She scrunched up her nose. "He decided me making contact with Dorrance couldn't hurt anything. It's not like the guy doesn't already hate my guts."

If she'd meant that to be funny, she'd missed her mark. Knowing a man as vicious as Gene Dorrance fully intended to punish Melinda in the worst of ways stayed with Boyd like an untreated wound, present whether he was waking and sleeping.

He only grunted and focused on splitting and buttering a biscuit.

"I thought I'd wait until morning," she said after a minute.

She'd dished up a lot of greens and only a small helping of casserole, he saw. He didn't expect her to have an appetite like his, but she'd visibly lost weight in barely over a week. She hadn't learned, as most soldiers did, that you had to shovel the food in when you could.

"Try one of these." He lifted his half-eaten biscuit. "They're really good."

She did and ate it with enthusiasm before picking up her fork to start on the rest of her meal.

You can lead a horse to water... he thought and concentrated on filling his own stomach.

"Does Gabe know what's going on?" she asked.

"Everyone in the county knows what's going on unless they don't follow the news at all. But yeah, I've put him and Leon on alert. A couple of other guys, too," he added.

Looking interested, she asked, "Veterans?"

"We hire a lot of them. You know that." Feeling some amusement, he said, "We're going to be hosting another guy shortly. I don't know if he's interested in ranching, but he needs someplace to stay while he gets his head together."

She cocked her head in interest.

Despite the rage of feelings he kept contained, Boyd grinned. "Should be fun. Joseph Marr is Trina's brother. He's a former teammate of mine and Gabe's. Hasn't made it here for a visit yet. Gabe's still feeling a little squeamish about taking Joseph's sister to bed every night knowing her brother is in the guest room."

"They're married!"

"Sure, but I bet they weren't the first time."

"What's he going to do, punch Gabe?"

"You never know. If so, I'm sure Gabe won't fight back."

Shaking her head, Melinda said in obvious disgust, *"Men."*

Boyd laughed.

Melinda kept eating, even helping herself to a second sourdough biscuit. Getting her thinking about something else had its rewards.

But her distraction lasted only so long. She balled up her napkin and looked at him, the bleakness back in her eyes.

"I wish we had a plan for tomorrow."

Boyd wished they had a plan at all. They'd started with one, but the only part that had paid off was the news barrage and the tip line. Now they were back to ground zero, without the faintest idea where Dorrance was holed up, or who he'd go after next.

And at the forefront of Boyd's thoughts was the wish that he could at least spend tonight wrapped around Melinda while they slept.

Keeping her safe from everyone but him.

MELINDA WAS SURE the meal had been delicious—she knew those sourdough biscuits were—but her mind hadn't been on food. She kept jumping between Dorrance and the horrors he'd perpetuated and might yet loose on someone else, and Boyd. The man who'd somehow persuaded her to come stay at his house, and who'd suggested she stay for good. Somehow, that subject hadn't come up again.

She almost rolled her eyes. She was a coward, that's why she hadn't confronted him right away. Well, and they'd been a little busy, too.

She wasn't used to feeling uncertain or...vulnerable. Emotionally *and* physically. If not for the emotional part, she wouldn't have hesitated to jump into bed with Boyd tonight. *He* wouldn't be likely to object. Her real trouble was that their lovemaking had been so far out of her previous experience, she'd never been able to think of it as just sex.

So if she made that choice, she'd be opening herself to a lot more than sharing her body and enjoying the pleasure of the moment. Did she trust him enough to do that?

She tuned in to find that, as was too often the case, he was watching her. God forbid he read her mind!

Feeling too antsy to just sit under the force of that thoughtful gaze, Melinda leaped up and began gathering dishes to carry to the sink. In a more leisurely way, Boyd did the same, but once he opened the dishwasher and started rinsing his plate, he said, "Why don't you let me finish up here?"

"You cooked." Her cheeks warmed. "Well, pushed buttons on the microwave."

He grinned with the deceptively lazy charm that had sucked her in the first time they met. "I'm good at that."

"I'm sure you are. But you're the one who labored hard today while all I did was stand around."

The humor left his face. "Bet you didn't like to be sidelined."

"No, I didn't, but—" Feeling awkward, she shrugged. "Obviously, I'm a little lacking in brawn."

A nerve in his cheek ticked. "You're not lacking in anything from where I stand."

Hearing the roughness in his voice, she grasped for the nerve to say, *I might have been wrong*.

What came out was, "I missed you."

"God, Melinda." The plate he'd held in his hand clattered into the sink and he turned off the flow of water with a single jab. "It's been killing me."

"You...you mean that?"

"Can you doubt it?"

Seeing the fire in his eyes, she didn't, even though she wasn't the most beautiful woman ever, never worked to make herself sexier for any man's sake, and had tried harder to fit in with the guys than she had to lure anyone like Boyd. And yet the first time he'd set eyes on her, he'd wanted her and she hadn't been able to help being just as drawn to him.

Swallowing, she shook her head and took a step toward him.

The next moment, his arms closed hard around her and his mouth found hers.

This kiss had a quality of desperation she'd never felt from him before or felt herself. There was nothing skilled about it. They kissed deeply, passionately, their bodies straining together. She dug her fingers into his shoulders to hold on, to lift herself to meet him.

He yanked his mouth away to kiss his way down her throat. Along the way, he mumbled, "I was trying so hard not to push you tonight."

"Why?" she whispered.

Boyd lifted his head to stare at her. "You've had a hellish few days, that's why."

"Maybe that's why I need you now," she said simply.

He groaned and said, "Screw the kitchen. Let's go upstairs."

They held hands again. This time, it felt symbolic, although probably she was making too much of what could turn out to be no more than a passionate, satisfying night.

Uh-huh. She couldn't forget what he'd said.

As far as I'm concerned, you don't need to figure anything out. I have in mind you staying for good.

Rational thought ended as soon as Boyd had hustled her into his bedroom. Next to the massive bed, he started stripping her. Even as her shirt and bra dropped to the floor, she wrenched at his shirt until he let her pull it over his head. She was hungry to see him naked, too. Her knees weakened at the sight of a powerful chest with just enough dark hair to almost hide his nipples, and then there was the muscle-rippled belly. She pressed her lips to the hollow at the base of his throat, then slid them downward. Just rubbing her cheek on his pecs sent a rush of pleasure through her.

He growled something under his breath, swung her up in his arms and laid her back on the bed. Before she could sit up, he peeled off the yoga pants and panties she'd found in her room.

She whimpered at the expression on his face as he raked his gaze over her. He made her feel beautiful, whether she was or not.

"You, too," she whispered and did sit up.

His dark eyes flicked to hers, and his hands went to the waist of his worn jeans. She was stunned to see that they shook. Even so, he shed jeans and his boxers so quick, her gaze didn't make it lower than the jutting evidence of his arousal. She reached for him, but he shook his head and backed away before fumbling at the bedside drawer.

"Let me—"

"I'm on birth control." Before, she'd insisted he use a condom, too.

His stare all but blistered her. "You're sure?"

Melinda bobbed her head.

She might as well have sliced the tether holding him back, because he was on her faster than she'd known he could move. Kissing her, then closing his mouth on first one breast, then the other. Licking, suckling, his unshaven cheek adding another sensation. His hands wandered, squeezing her hips, before one traced a path to the junction of her thighs. Once his fingers slid into her slick folds, she was lost. All she wanted was him, and she wanted him *now*.

As big and solid as he was, she wouldn't have been able to move him until he was damn well good and ready, but apparently he was, because suddenly his knees pushed hers apart and he was there, between her legs. Pressing against her, taunting her, then pushing slowly inside. A huge shudder shook him. And all the while, he watched her.

She moaned. Her back arched in a near spasm, and she used her hands and even fingernails to urge him on. "Now. Please. Now."

He surged into her, sinking himself deep, and for the first time closed his eyes. "So good," he muttered.

Better than she remembered, and that was saying a lot. She'd never needed anyone like this, but he was there, filling her, driving her up. Her back arched, and the excruciating coil of tension broke, flooding her with pleasure and joy.

She cried his name, and felt his body jerk as he came, too, pulsing inside her. She barely heard her name as he whispered it against her neck.

Chapter Sixteen

Sprawled on his back with Melinda wrapped in his arms and her head on his shoulder, Boyd felt amazing. The best in a long time. Ever, maybe. He'd been so afraid they'd never get here again—

She stirred. "That was—"

He lifted his head slightly, but still couldn't see much of her face. "Out of this world?"

Her chuckle vibrated against his side and chest, making him think he might be ready for round two without much of a break.

"Maybe," she murmured. "Only...this doesn't mean—"

Hearing the return to wariness in her tone, Boyd's excellent mood evaporated and his whole body stiffened. "Mean what?"

"You don't have to sound hostile!"

"No?" He reared up, dumping her onto the bed. "We've just made love, and you're already stringing the barbed wire? How am I supposed to take that?"

She sat up, too, eyes wide, silky dark hair tangling

around her face and shoulders. "That's not what I was trying to say."

"Then what *did* you intend to say?" He wasn't doing himself any favors, but was too pissed to rein himself in. Damn it, having her pull back before he'd even caught his breath hurt.

Melinda raised her firm chin. "I'm nervous, that's all. Okay? I'm not quite ready to…to move in yet, even if you seem to think it's that easy!"

He winced at the reminder. She, of all women, had been guaranteed to hate the way he'd tossed out his intentions. Releasing a long breath, Boyd reached to cup her jaw and cheek. To his relief, she tipped her head enough to nestle her face in his palm.

"I know it's not that easy," he said quietly. "When I said that, I was letting you know what I want. I didn't do it very well."

"No kidding." Her forehead puckered. "I don't get it. Every time I see you on TV, you're so…charming. Every woman in your vicinity starts blushing and smiling."

"Would that work with you?"

She stared at him for an uncomfortable moment, not so much as blinking. "Not once I saw through it. I mean, sure, you mowed me right over when we first met. But after you blew it, I realized that I was never sure how deep those smiles went."

"I'm sorry."

She frowned. "It's more than that. Did you ever really pay attention to me? Did you have the slightest idea who I was?"

"Of course I did. Why else would I be so irrational? You scared me—"

"Because of Raquel." She remembered his girlfriend's name. Of course she did.

He cleared his throat. "Yeah. I'm still afraid for you. Back then, I overreacted. Granger County wasn't exactly a war zone."

"But now it is," she said, a little wryly.

"Seems that way, doesn't it?"

In her unnerving way, she studied him for a minute. He dreaded what was to come. He'd never figured out how Gabe, notoriously closemouthed, had engineered a romance with Trina. Maybe being a therapist had taught her how to coax words—and meaningful ones, at that—from a stone.

Unfortunately, it was true that Boyd knew how to charm people on one level, but when it got to anything as raw as emotions, he was as bad as his partner. What she saw on his face right now, he couldn't conceive.

"I love being here with you," she said, surprising him. "Not just in bed." She looked a little shy. "Eating dinner together, talking about our days. You know."

He knew.

"I just…need to be able to trust that you'll understand when I make the decisions I do. And back me up when I need it. Not…assume you know best."

"Have I done that since Dorrance showed up in town? Or earlier when we arrested the bank robbers?"

Her lashes fluttered a few times, as if he'd surprised her. "No," she said finally, "but for most of the time I assumed that was because you didn't have any particular interest in me anymore."

"You assumed wrong," he said gruffly. "I didn't know if you'd give me the time of day, but in the back of my mind, I never quit hoping."

Was that a shimmer in her eyes?

"Then why…?"

"Didn't I charge after you?"

Her head bobbed.

"Partly—" Boyd rubbed a hand over his face. That hand was shaking. He didn't like having no control over whether she decided in his favor or not.

What's more, this much honesty didn't come easily for him. Raquel aside, he'd never had a serious relationship with a woman. Short-term hookups, sure. His most important, lasting friendships were with friends and teammates, but the boys and men he knew, and perhaps especially soldiers, they didn't talk out how they felt the same way. Or at all.

He had to start again. "Partly, it was the way you looked at me with such astonishment and then dismissal. You walked out as if you hadn't been that invested anyway." That had felt like taking a slug to his chest. Maybe he'd been wearing a vest so he wasn't bleeding to death, but that didn't protect him from pain. He forced himself to keep talking, however little he liked doing it. "Then I'd made that vow. I've had some ugly wounds in my years in the army, but nothing that hurt like hearing Raquel was dead. I was looking forward to seeing her, then *wham*. I

was convinced I couldn't go through that again. I...
didn't see yet that I'd fallen for her, and then you,
because you were strong women. Warriors. And if I
loved you, I had to accept your job instead of treat-
ing it like a nine-to-five you could quit in favor of
doing something else."

"It took you years to reach that epiphany?"

He grimaced. "I was getting there when we
worked that serial killer investigation together. But
Daniel and Lindsay came so close to being killed.
That could have been you."

"So you chickened out again."

It was more complicated than that, but he chose
not to remind her how open she'd been with her dislike of him. If she'd betrayed any suggestion that
she'd missed him...

"What about next time?" she challenged him.

"This *is* next time. I haven't gotten in the way of
you doing your job, have I?"

"No. That's why I came home with you, you
know."

He smiled crookedly. "Although you made sure
you had your own car here."

"Seemed smart." She scooted closer to him on
the mattress, not quite closing the distance, but getting there. "I'm sorry I started this. I guess I just..."

At her hesitation, Boyd finished her sentence,
"Aren't sure you trust me."

Her eyes searched his. "I'm not very good at trust.
You know that."

"I know." A ragged sound escaped him. "Come here. I wasn't done with you."

Would never be done with her.

He'd imagined progressing to slow and tender once they'd eased that first frantic need, but their little talk had him feeling as if his horse had just bolted at the same moment he'd realized the girth of the saddle was loose. The need to join with her, and *now*, roared back to life.

Thank God, she met his mouth with just as much intensity and passion.

MELINDA STOOD ON the front porch that stretched the entire width of the huge log house and watched Boyd's black department SUV recede down the ranch road. She kind of wished she'd gone with him; he would have preferred to drop her at the police station and come back for her after he'd finished his business at the sheriff's headquarters. He'd gone back and forth on that, though.

"If you're there at the station, you'd head out with Daniel or any other officer in a minute, wouldn't you?" he'd said. "I think Dorrance has to be planning another ambush. You should be safe here." He'd sighed at that point. "You don't have to tell me that I'm being protective. Not sure how much I can change."

If he could accept her, she had to accept him as well: a former officer and soldier who'd spent years in war zones. He had a way of making her feel safe, too. But as far as today went, she refused to be afraid to be left alone. This was about her, not Boyd. His housekeeper wasn't scheduled to work today, which meant she'd be alone here for however many hours Boyd was gone.

"Do your job," Boyd had said tersely, although his final words were, "I've got Gabe on alert. He and Leon will be somewhere on the ranch and carrying phones."

He'd input both of their numbers into her phone.

Now, heeding his insistence, she went back inside and locked the dead bolt on the front door.

The plan was for her to respond to any calls to the tip line that seemed worthy of follow-up. Maybe from the sheriff's department, too; she didn't know. Boyd's business was apparently administrative, not surprising given how little time he'd spent at his desk this past week or more. She knew he was going to start by firing a deputy. He was mad to have to do it when his small force was already stretched so thin, but negligence couldn't be excused.

Melinda wandered into the kitchen, a room made airy by large expanses of windows looking out on ponderosa or lodgepole pine woods and pastures.

She poured herself a second cup of coffee and sipped it standing right in front of the expanse of windows, smiling despite herself as she watched several older foals bucking and chasing each other along the fence line.

The phone she'd just set down on the counter beeped and gave a little bounce to let her know a text had arrived. She stiffened. There'd been no response to the one she'd sent Dorrance earlier that morning. If it was him—

It was, with an attached photo. A girl with terrified eyes.

Chloe Decker, the adopted daughter of Boyd's partner, Gabe. A child who'd survived seeing her family butchered. Sickened, Melinda scanned the text itself.

I'm watching you. If you try to forward this text or make a call, I'll kill the kid. Drop your phone. NOW. Walk out the back door.

For a fraction of an instance, her fingers tightened. Would he really see if she took the brief moment it would take to send this to Boyd, who might not even have turned out onto the highway yet?

But movement outside drew her eyes, and she saw a man standing not that far away between tall pines. He had a child slung over his shoulder, and a handgun.

Melinda let the phone clatter to the floor.

MAN, HE DIDN'T like leaving her. During their careful discussion, Boyd had hidden the depths of his fear and his paranoid belief he had to stay close to Melinda.

Even as he emerged onto the highway and accelerated southbound, he battled the need to turn back. What if she needed him? But what if she didn't, and

was insulted by his lack of faith in her ability to protect herself?

And, damn, what made him think that psycho
killer had managed to sneak onto the ranch and was
close enough to threaten Melinda, anyway?

Yeah, but he didn't believe Gene Dorrance was
holed up in a falling-down barn somewhere brooding and licking his wounds. He knew his time was
limited and intended to make the most of it.

He didn't seem to expect to survive unscathed
and go on to live a happy life in some other part of
the country. All he wanted was the people he hated
to pay for their crimes against him. He must see that
his options were increasingly limited, which meant
he'd want to be sure to degrade and murder Melinda
before he died himself.

Boyd's stomach clenched and his foot hovered
above the brake as he fought his instincts.

He'd laid his phone on the console between seats
to be sure he didn't miss any important calls or texts.
Even as he forced himself to drive on, he kept flicking glances at it, suspicious of the silence. He'd give
a lot to be on horseback somewhere on the ranch,
Melinda riding beside him. No crime on their minds.
He'd begun to hate this stint as sheriff, except what if
he hadn't pinned on the badge, giving him the ability to support and protect her?

If he failed—

The damn phone rang. Not dispatch or one of his
deputies. The caller was Gabe Decker. It would take

more than an everyday problem on the ranch for his partner to need to consult with him right now.

"Gabe?"

"Chloe is missing." His voice was taut, agony thinly suppressed. "This isn't like her. Trina just called. I'm fifteen minutes away from home. Any chance you're closer?"

Fear squeezed Boyd's rib cage. He braked, keeping an eye on his rearview mirror. "Yeah. Hell. I left Melinda alone at the house."

"You don't think—?"

Boyd recognized the sudden sharpness in his partner's voice. He'd heard it when they were under pressure in dire circumstances. Yeah, Boyd did think, and Gabe was seeing the same terrifying possibilities.

"Tell Trina not to go anywhere near my place," Boyd snapped, and dropped the phone back onto the console even as his speed dropped to a point where he was able to wrench the steering wheel into a U-turn. The tires squealed, and he burned rubber as he stomped on the gas to speed back to the ranch.

The battle-ready part of him calculated despite the fear that could have paralyzed him.

He'd have to park well before he reached the house. Given the lack of rain, he'd raise a plume of dirt once he hit the ranch road. Thank God he had his rifle with him.

He picked up the phone again and dialed Leon. When his foreman answered, Boyd asked, "Where are you?"

"Gabe already called. I'm on my way in, but not close enough to help if anything goes down in the next ten, fifteen minutes."

"Do your best."

Boyd's hand clenched on the phone. *Call Melinda*, he decided.

She didn't answer. She could be on a call made because of the tip line, thinking she could get back to him. He tried again, listened to ring after ring until her voice mail picked up.

Again.

No answer.

Dorrance had figured out how to get to Melinda, Boyd knew with icy certainty. Another child, a young girl again, and this time one Melinda already knew, although Dorrance probably wasn't aware of that. Didn't matter to him; he'd figured out her Achilles' heel.

Back on the packed dirt road, Boyd hardly slowed down. A pothole he hadn't noticed before threw the SUV sideways, but he controlled it with a steady hand. There was the turnoff to Gabe's cabin; time to ditch the vehicle and proceed on foot.

He suddenly wished like hell that Joseph Marr had arrived to provide backup. Gabe would have said if he had.

Boyd gave brief thought to where Dorrance had hidden his car. Then he dismissed the issue. Didn't matter; Dorrance would be on foot now.

He'd have grabbed Chloe, maybe gone so far as to knock her out so she couldn't scream and alert her mother, who handled a handgun or rifle with impressive competence thanks to her army ranger brother's insistence. Trina had proved able to shoot to kill, if that's what it took to protect someone she loved. Boyd had no doubt she had a weapon in hand right now, but she didn't have the skills he could have used to corner Dorrance.

Boyd drove off the road into a stand of pine trees. Some minor undergrowth didn't hide the SUV, but made it less obvious. Dorrance wasn't that close, though. With Melinda not answering her phone—

Even as he took out his rifle and checked to be sure it was ready to fire, Boyd had to fight not to succumb to the tornado of terror and anguish that could have whipped him away. If there'd ever been a battle he had to win, this was it.

For Melinda, and for the cute kid Gabe and Trina loved so much.

Boyd broke into a run.

MELINDA SHUDDERED. Her sidearm in its holster lay on the table where she'd imagined being able to grab it quickly. But he could see her clearly through the windows. If she diverted on her way to the door, Dorrance would see.

And…she felt sure he'd search her when she reached him. If he kept the barrel of his own gun pressed to Chloe's head, she wouldn't dare open fire.

All she could do was walk out that back door, hands in the air and pray she had a chance to fight back. He despised women. Might he underestimate her, be unable to imagine any female having the ability to overcome him?

Andrea had, she reminded herself—but so momentarily, Dorrance was likely to discount her courage and strength.

If worse came to worst, Melinda could only hope he'd let Chloe go. Gripped by anguish as she accepted the likelihood of her own death, she saw Boyd's face as he'd looked down at her while they made love. The wanting, the tenderness, the commitment. She couldn't have imagined seeing that. If he lost another woman he loved to violence—

Don't think about it. Do what you have to do.

She opened the door and walked out onto the deck, hands in the air.

Chapter Seventeen

Boyd scanned the landscape ahead and to the sides even as he sprinted full out. Reason said Dorrance wouldn't have knocked on the front door. He'd use Chloe to lure Melinda out back, however he accomplished it. He'd obviously waited until Boyd left, so he'd been somewhere he could identify the black SUV as it receded, watch the dust plume all the way out to the highway.

Not hard to do.

What was his intention? To kill Melinda immediately to ensure he got it done, that he could have the chance to watch the light leave her eyes? Or was he set on having time with her? Long enough to reduce her to a broken excuse for the woman she was, to make her beg?

He was deluding himself if he thought Melinda McIntosh would ever beg for her life. But then, nobody could say Dorrance was sane.

If that's what he wanted, he had to have a spot picked out that he believed would give him privacy for a few minutes to a few hours. One of the unoccupied cabins? An outbuilding that was unlocked, or that he'd been able to break into?

Boyd had to believe Dorrance wouldn't go for a quick death for the woman he hated so much. Because if he did, a gunshot would split the quiet day any minute, ending her life.

The house reared ahead.

HANDS SPREAD OPEN so Dorrance could see that she didn't carry either her phone or a weapon, Melinda walked as slowly as she could without being too obvious. She'd opened her every sense, watching for any tiny flicker of movement to one side or the other, the steady clop of a horse's hooves or the engine of a ranch vehicle on the road. A voice. Anything at all that might distract Dorrance...or give her hope that she wasn't alone confronting him.

But the quiet was so absolute, even eerie, she wondered where the birds had gone. Even the yearlings she'd earlier watched running grazed now. As she neared the trees, reddish soil puffed under her every footstep.

Dorrance waited where she'd first seen him. A child lay limp over his shoulder. Not "a child": Chloe. Fine, strawberry blond hair spilled down his chest.

He looked different, she saw, as soon as she was near enough to study him. She'd been right about the weight lifting; despite the added years, he'd become considerably brawnier than he was that day in the courtroom. He'd gone completely gray, though, and his hair was thinning. She doubted he cared.

His eyes burned as he watched her approach. Melinda doubted he'd had a thought that didn't have to do with revenge in the intervening years. That hate twisted his face into ugliness.

He was also filthy, which wasn't a surprise after he'd lost his access to a shower and washing machine and dryer. Had he managed to find anything to eat? She hoped not. Hunger would weaken him.

She stopped twenty feet away from him. "I'm here. Let the kid go."

"You're not that stupid. Keep walking. You need to pass me. Go straight ahead. I'll follow behind you."

Melinda wanted to cast a glance over her shoulder. Oh, God, why had she talked Boyd into leaving?

Dorrance would only have waited. Or, if his ploy to use Chloe had failed, he might have killed her and dumped the body.

In sudden horror, Melinda wondered: Was Chloe alive? She hung so limply, Melinda couldn't be sure. *Please, let her only be unconscious.* That might be best. It would…protect her from knowing what was happening. She'd suffered enough horror for a lifetime when she'd seen her family murdered.

Melinda's skin crawled as she passed within a couple of feet of Dorrance. Walking forward with him behind her, unable to see him, was worse. The prickling up and down the back of her neck could have been the path of a scorpion searching for the right place to sting. She couldn't forget the hank of graying brown hair he'd used to taunt her. Would he cut hers off right away?

There was no path, but undergrowth was scanty here on the far edge of forests that covered the eastern side of the Cascade Mountains. The heat and dry climate had a big impact. What clumps she saw of bitterbrush, snowberry, wax currant and Oregon grape were easy to avoid.

Would Dorrance notice if she "accidentally" stepped on a plant and broke a few branches? Would he realize she was trying to lay a trail?

Dorrance ordered her to continue straight ahead. She caught a glimpse from the corner of her eye of the fence line off to her left. They seemed to be paralleling it.

Behind her, she heard a crunching sound and a growl. He had stepped on something like the low-growing pinemat manzanita.

"Hands up!" he snapped, and she realized she'd let her arms sag.

Melinda's fingers were tingling, ready to go numb, but she forced her hands higher again.

Where was he taking her?

BOYD WAS FORCED to slow his pace before he reached the house. He circled around it, easing from one bit of cover to another. He couldn't disappear here as training and experience allowed him to in a lusher landscape or a sunbaked adobe town with crooked streets, but he studied his surroundings carefully each time before he moved.

He came into sight of the deck—and the back door, standing open as Melinda must have left it. Unless Dorrance had gone *in*, thinking he'd have long enough before anyone came looking?

Boyd's gut said no. He must realize that Chloe's disappearance would be noted quickly. If Gabe had been home and learned that Melinda was here alone, he'd have searched the house after she didn't answer the door.

Boyd sifted through other possibilities, not liking how many there were even with Dorrance and Melinda on foot.

First the garage and then, a quarter of a mile farther, the long string of cabins built for ranch employees lay to the north of the house. There were a couple of empty cabins right now—but Dorrance would take an enormous risk of being seen if he tried to use one. In normal times, as a stranger he might not have occasioned comment, since ranch hands came and went seasonally, but his photo had been spread far and wide. A man carrying a child and either holding a gun on that child or a woman?

He'd need space and privacy. The woods here weren't dense—this land had all been logged at one point—but they extended for several miles. Some minor ranch roads crisscrossed through the second-growth forest, but Boyd and Gabe had made the decision not to log. They had enough pasture. As a result, not much lay this way…but finding Dorrance and Melinda among the trees might be like searching for the needle in a haystack.

And, damn, ideally he'd spot them somewhere he

could set up a shot—and get it off before Dorrance could pull the trigger to kill Melinda or Chloe.

If Chloe was still alive.

Boyd gave his head a sharp shake. He couldn't afford to think like that.

Slipping from tree to tree, wishing these trunks were large enough to truly hide a man his size, he watched for footprints or any other sign that someone had passed this way recently. Too bad the earth was dry and hard right now.

Wait. His thoughts snapped to a stop. *Haystack.* Hay.

There were a couple of decrepit cabins out here, part of the ranch's past. One was close to falling down—maybe had. Boyd hadn't had reason to pass it since winter. But they'd done enough repairs on the other cabin to use it as a hay shed. A narrow track led to it from the main ranch road so that bales of hay could be unloaded and stored there. One of the feeding stations for the horses was just on the other side of the fence.

If Dorrance had explored… Yeah, that was a good possibility. If he knew anything about ranching, he'd be aware that horses and cattle both mainly relied on pasture at this time of year. Late summer or early fall, when the grasses were dry or grazed down, Boyd or Gabe would make the decision to start supplementing the stock's diet, while making sure they had enough hay to last through the winter.

Wary of focusing too quickly on one site, Boyd nevertheless kept moving that way. It made sense.

And then he saw some crushed vegetation.

SHE COULD HARDLY feel her arms and hands. Even if she could get her hands on a weapon, would she be able to use it effectively, or be so blasted stiff and clumsy she'd drop anything she tried to grab?

Uh-huh. And what weapon would that be? She hadn't seen even a fallen branch solid enough to be useful.

Once she turned her head to try to get a look over her shoulder.

A low, menacing voice said, "You think I won't kill her?"

No, Melinda knew better than that. This man lacked any pretense at a conscience or sense of empathy. Although he wouldn't want to shoot—that would draw attention. He wouldn't have to, though; he could break a five-year-old girl's neck with a quick wrench of his hands.

She hoped he didn't see her shudder. He craved her fear, which meant she couldn't betray any.

Where are you, Boyd?

Had anyone noticed Chloe's absence yet? Midmorning like this, Melinda would expect so. Nap time might have been different.

What would Dorrance have done if Boyd hadn't left? she found herself wondering again. Or if she'd gone with him? Hidden with Chloe, thinking a chance would come? Or killed her, shrugged and dreamed up another strategy while he bided his time?

She heard a whimper.

Chloe. That had to be Chloe.

"Shut up!"

She was alive.

The exhilarating knowledge buzzed under Melinda's skin, energizing her. Whatever else happened, she had to save the little girl.

If only determination was enough.

Just ahead, a tree root had pushed the soil up. She deliberately stepped wrong on it, stumbled and fell into a bush before hitting the trunk of a ponderosa pine and scraping her knuckles over it.

Dorrance stopped. "Get back out here. And don't do that again." Teeth showing, he jiggled Chloe. "Or I might not bother hauling her along any farther."

Cheek on Dorrance's chest, Chloe had opened her blue eyes and was watching, although she looked dazed.

Don't fight, Melinda wanted to beg, even though Chloe could provide the distraction that would allow her to jump him. It was too dangerous, though, and a child her age too fragile.

She pushed her way back through the thin branches of what she thought was a snowberry or maybe a huckleberry bush and pretended to limp once she stepped free.

"Go."

BOYD DEBATED TEXTING Leon and Gabe to let them know where he was, but as much as he'd have liked backup, he made the decision not to. The sudden appearance of one or the other of the men could precipitate a crisis, and potentially a bloodbath. If he thought either had been close enough, he'd have asked them to advance up the dirt track to the hay shed, but by the time they circled around…no. Right now, the best chance was for him to see Dorrance ahead and get a good, clear shot.

He carried his rifle in his left hand and his Glock in his right. Just in case he stumbled on them unexpectedly he had to be prepared, but he would prefer that not happen. He moved as fast as he thought he could without screwing up, setting each foot down with care to be sure not even a twig snapped under his weight.

The unnatural silence made him believe they weren't far ahead, certainly near enough to make the birds and small mammals wary. That didn't mean they hadn't veered to the southwest. Not to the southeast; Dorrance was unlikely to steer them any closer to the fence, where they might become visible to a ranch hand on horseback—or, although he didn't know it, to either Decker or Leon Cabrera, both riding hard to get back.

Not having seen the fence in a while, Boyd began to worry about whether he was still following behind his quarry. Dodging from one bit of cover to another, it would be easy to deviate from a direct line. He wished like hell Melinda could have left a few more breadcrumbs in her path. Or had she, and he'd missed them?

He stood still and carefully examined every bit of undergrowth within a wide radius. Relief hit when he saw the broken whippets on a clump of the ubiquitous common snowberry. Closing in on it, Boyd zeroed in on what he'd swear was a smear of blood higher than he'd expect on the rough trunk of the pine. Would she have reached up to break her fall?

His heart clenched. God—what if the blood was from a previous injury?

It couldn't be severe, he told himself, or she wouldn't still be walking—and still be able to leave him a signpost.

He shouldn't have doubted her.

He continued forward, a ghost slipping through the dry forest. He didn't think the hay shed was far ahead. If that wasn't Dorrance's goal... Boyd didn't let himself dwell on the might or might not be. At the least, the old log building would provide excellent concealment.

A growl of sound had him freezing in place. Was that a voice? If so, it had to be Dorrance's.

Boyd slid from the cover of one tree to another, his every sense focused on the origin of that sound. He let himself move a little faster than he had been, knowing time had slowed in that way it had during action. He couldn't count on Gabe or Leon.

A faint squeak came to his ears next. Hinges. He increased his pace. Once Dorrance got Melinda and Chloe stashed deep in the shed, it might be impossible to take him out before he could pull his own trigger.

THE CABIN LOOKED like the kind of place Dorrance could have hidden the past few days. A small-paned window in the side couldn't have been washed in years—decades—but let Melinda see what she thought was a heap of hay bales.

"Open the door," he ordered.

No padlock. She turned the hasp and swung open one of the double doors that looked newer than the structure itself. The interior was murky, daylight not reaching far inside the limited opening. Yes, she'd been right about the hay, stacked high and nearly filling the entire space. If there'd once been walls or a loft, they'd been removed.

"Don't suppose anybody will be tossing out hay for the horses today," Dorrance said, sounding almost genial. He waved the gun toward her. "In."

"I know you don't want to kill a child," she said, as steadily as she could manage. "Why don't you leave her out here?"

"So she can run for help?"

"She wouldn't have any idea where to go. She's only five."

"You know her."

Betraying that much had been a mistake.

She shrugged. "I recognize her. She saw her family murdered a couple of years ago. I have no idea if she's anywhere near recovered from that tragedy yet."

"Isn't that interesting?" Dorrance sounded pleased. "Won't take much effort to bring her to heel then, will it?"

Sickened but hiding it, Melinda said, "You've never gone for children."

He shrugged. "You're right, but she's useful. It's your fault I needed her."

"Oh, bull." She let him see her contempt—but not, she prayed, her terror. "You make your own decisions."

His eyes narrowed and he ground the barrel of the Glock into Chloe's temple again. "Now, do what I tell you!"

She'd irritated him, maybe rocked him slightly off balance. If he'd just turn the gun away from Chloe, Melinda would take any chance to jump him.

"Up," he snarled.

The hay had been stacked in a crude stairsteps. As she clambered atop the first level, two bales high, she heard tiny, scuttling sounds. Mice. Would he freak if one ran across his foot? Shoot at it?

Height gave her an advantage, didn't it? As she climbed atop the next stack, yet another two bales high, she crawled closer to the window. If there were any others, they'd been blocked by the hay. At least this one gave her some light.

The door swung closed behind her, until that small dirty window provided the only illumination, and it was murky.

He tossed Chloe atop the first level and then swung the gun to point at Melinda. "Sit down."

Oh, God, oh, God.

BOTH DOORS WERE CLOSED, although from inside Dorrance wouldn't be able to turn the hasp to secure them. Since they swung outward, he wouldn't have any way to lock them, either. Boyd didn't like the odds of that kind of frontal assault, though.

Fighting to suppress all emotion, needing right now to be a soldier, not a man who loved the kidnap victim, he evaluated the old cabin to determine his best option. He could wait until he had backup, but given that there was only one way in or out of the place, that might not help. And what would Melinda and Chloe suffer during that extra ten or fifteen minutes?

Would Melinda have any chance to make a move?

He couldn't depend on that, but had no doubt she'd fight. That scared him as nothing else could, but he also had faith she'd use her head.

That was the moment he saw movement inside the window. Not clear, but he knew it was Melinda. Standing? Kneeling? Hard to tell. A sinking feeling told him *this* might be his only good chance. But unable to see through the scum and dirt covering the glass increased the risk of him shooting the wrong person.

He closed his eyes for a moment, then holstered the handgun and lifted the rifle to evaluate distance. There wasn't even a breeze he had to account for. The moment he pressed his eye socket to the scope, the small square of the window leaped into focus.

He lowered the rifle and glanced around. If he could find a branch low enough to rest it on, he'd eliminate any possible tremor in his hands or arms.

He saw a jagged Y thrusting out from a pine where a branch had broken off. A little bit more of an angle to the window than from here, but not so much it should make a different.

Now to drag out some facsimile of the clear-headed and dispassionate patience that had once come so naturally to him in combat situations. If only Melinda could know he was here, waiting for that psycho to show his head in the window.

IF HE CONCENTRATED on her, he'd forget Chloe. Would the girl think to shove open the door and run? If she did, would he react fast enough to gun her down?

"Take off your shirt."

Melinda reluctantly peeled her shirt over her head, hating the creepy way Dorrance watched her.

"Now the bra." She wanted him to forget Chloe. If he climbed up here, she had a chance of wrestling his arm to one side or even kicking the gun from his hand. Or...

Boyd, Gabe Decker and Leon Cabrera were all army-trained snipers. Even Daniel was. If there was any chance at all that one of them had tracked her and Dorrance to this cabin, they might conceivably be able to take a shot through the window.

Dream on.

God help her. Moving very, very slowly, she reached behind her. "Not a chance."

He ate her up with lust-filled eyes, apparently assuming she'd obey. "How does it feel, filling in for Andrea and Erica? Sometimes they even enjoyed themselves, you know."

"I doubt that." Her voice shook despite her best effort. But with an abrupt movement, he hoisted himself up the stacked bales and over her, using his weight to press her down onto the scratchy bed of hay. He dropped the gun, but suddenly he had a wicked looking knife in his hand.

He was excited, mumbling something about her jeans—and maybe carving her up some, just to let her know how powerless she was. He hadn't pinned her arms, though, probably discounting her ability to fight back.

Out of the corner of her eye, she saw movement. Chloe. Not going for the gun, but slipping off the hay bales. Yes! Melinda would lose in a battle of strength with Dorrance, but she wouldn't submit without fighting back, and a distraction might give her a momentary advantage.

The door swung open. With a bellow of rage, he turned his head—and Melinda slammed the heels of her hands into his throat. She forced his head up, up, even as he lifted the knife.

And then his head exploded, just as she heard the crack of a rifle.

Sprayed with blood, soaked with it, she shoved him off her, seeing his body bounce down the stair-steps of hay bales.

Only a second later, Boyd appeared in the open doorway.

Epilogue

It was close to an hour before Boyd was free to go home. He'd fired the kill shot and had to account for his choices to Daniel, the first cop to show up. The few questions had been pro forma, though; Daniel wasn't seriously questioning Boyd's recitation of events or his decision to pull the trigger.

He wasn't the only one who was so relieved, his knees shook like a newborn foal's. Gabe held on to Chloe like he'd never let go again.

The paramedic had felt the lump on her head and gazed into her eyes with a scope before deciding to transport her to the hospital.

Gabe rose to his feet with the five-year-old looking tiny in his arms. "I'm going with her."

Nobody argued.

By that time Leon had walked Melinda to the house. She'd yanked her T-shirt over her head to mostly cover her bloody torso.

She sat at the kitchen table when he finally walked in, her fine-boned face marble white. She was clean, thank God, hair wet. He had to wonder how long she'd stayed in the shower. Whether she yet felt clean.

When she heard the back door open and saw him, she shoved back the chair and stood. He groaned, crossed the kitchen floor in three strides and yanked her into his arms. He knew exactly how Gabe felt. If he had his way, Melinda wouldn't leave his sight for weeks to come. He didn't care if she called him possessive.

"I've never been so scared in my life," he mumbled into that wet hair. "I love you. Realizing he had you—" The shudder was so powerful, he might have been ripped open by the San Andreas fault.

"I was afraid I'd never see you again," she whispered, making him realize she'd locked her arms around him and knotted the back of his shirt in her hands. "I told myself if only I could save Chloe—"

"You did. You did that." Around the lump in his throat, he told her the truth. "Unless he'd already killed her, I never had any doubt you'd find a way to set Chloe free."

Melinda lifted her head enough to see him. "Really?"

"Really." God, he sounded as if he'd used coarse sandpaper on his throat. Maybe all those internal screams had done the damage.

"I still feel gross."

"I'm sorry." Gentle didn't come easily right now; despite everything, he was aroused and she must know it. "If I could have gotten there sooner—"

Her eyes shimmered. "I thought you might be

out there. I still can't believe you really were." Her breath hitched. This astonishingly strong woman was crying.

"You've never been able to count on anyone."

Damp or not, her eyes held his. "I was wrong about you."

"Not as wrong as I was about you."

"Oh, Boyd." She buried her face against his neck again, but she didn't sob, just maintained her grip on him. Her knuckles dug into his back.

He pressed his cheek to the top of her head, closed his eyes and prepared to wait as long as he needed to. This was a different kind of patience, and he'd give her as much as she needed.

A long time later she sighed and released his shirt. She freed herself from his powerful embrace and studied him with those mesmerizing green-gold eyes.

"You...you really want me to stay here with you?"

"I want you to marry me. I want us to have kids when you're ready." He didn't so much as blink. "I swear I won't let you down."

Her smile was small and shaky. "I think you've proved yourself. I love you, too, you know. If I hadn't back then, you couldn't have hurt me so much."

"I will never forgive myself."

"I was just as dumb." Oddly, tears brimmed again in her eyes even as she took the step to close the distance between them again. "Do you know what I'd like?"

If it was an ice cream cone, or to be taken to the

hospital to see Chloe and Kristina, he'd give her what she wanted even if it killed him.

"What?" he asked roughly.

"I'd like you to make love with me. I need to see *you* looking at me so I can wipe out any memory of *him*."

Incapable of words, Boyd snatched her up in his arms and carried her to the staircase. She wrapped her arms around his neck and held on for the ride.

* * * * *

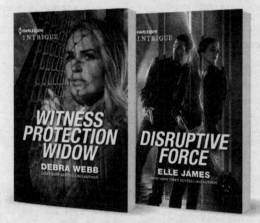

COMING NEXT MONTH FROM

⧫HARLEQUIN

INTRIGUE

#2061 MURDER GONE COLD
A Colt Brothers Investigation • by B.J. Daniels
When James Colt decides to solve his late father's final murder case, he has no idea it will implicate his high school crush Lorelei Wilkins's stepmother. Now James and Lorelei must unravel a cover-up involving some of the finest citizens of Lonesome, Montana...including a killer determined to keep the truth hidden.

#2062 DECOY TRAINING
K-9s on Patrol • by Caridad Piñeiro
Former marine Shane Adler's used to perilous situations. But he's stunned to find danger in the peaceful Idaho mountains—especially swirling around his beautiful dog trainer, Piper Lambert. It's up to Shane—and his loyal K-9 in training, Decoy—to make sure a mysterious enemy won't derail her new beginning...or his.

#2063 SETUP AT WHISKEY GULCH
The Outriders Series • by Elle James
After losing her fiancé to an IED explosion, sheriff's deputy Dallas Jones planned to start over in Whiskey Gulch. But when she finds herself in the middle of a murder investigation, Dallas partners with Outrider Levi Warren. Their investigation, riddled with gangs, drugs and death threats, sparks an unexpected attraction—one they may not survive.

#2064 GRIZZLY CREEK STANDOFF
Eagle Mountain: Search for Suspects • by Cindi Myers
When police deputy Ronin Doyle happens upon stunning Courtney Baker, he can't shake the feeling that something's not right. And as the lawman's engulfed by an investigation that rocks their serene community, more and more he's convinced that Courtney's boyfriend has swept her—and her beloved daughter—into something sinister...

#2065 ACCIDENTAL WITNESS
Heartland Heroes • by Julie Anne Lindsey
While searching for her missing roommate, Jen Jordan barely survives coming face-to-face with a gunman. Panicked, the headstrong mom enlists the help of Deputy Knox Winchester, her late fiancé's best friend, who will have to race against time to protect Jen and her baby...and expose the criminals putting all their lives in jeopardy.

#2066 GASLIGHTED IN COLORADO
by Cassie Miles
Deputy John Graystone vows to help Caroline McAllister recover her fractured memories of why she's covered in blood. As mounting evidence surrounds Caroline, a stalker arrives on the scene shooting from the shadows and leaving terrifying notes. Is John protecting—and falling for—an amnesiac victim being gaslighted...or is there more to this crime than he ever imagined?

YOU CAN FIND MORE INFORMATION ON UPCOMING HARLEQUIN TITLES, FREE EXCERPTS AND MORE AT HARLEQUIN.COM.

HICNM0222

SPECIAL EXCERPT FROM

HQN

*Bad things have been happening to Buckhorn residents,
and Darby Fulton's sure it has something to do with
a new store called Gossip. As a newspaper publisher,
she can't ignore the story, any more than she can resist
being drawn to former cop Jasper Cole.
Their investigation pulls them both into a twisted
scheme of revenge where secrets are a deadly weapon...*

Read on for a sneak preview of
Before Buckhorn,
part of the Buckhorn, Montana series,
by New York Times *bestselling author B.J. Daniels.*

Saturday evening the crows came. Jasper Cole looked
up from where he'd been standing in his ranch kitchen
cleaning up his dinner dishes. He'd heard the rustle of
feathers and looked up with a start to see several dozen
crows congregated on the telephone line outside.

Just the sight of them stirred a memory of a time
dozens of crows had come to his grandparents' farmhouse
when he was five. The chill he felt at both the memory
and the arrival of the crows had nothing to do with the
cool Montana spring air coming in through the kitchen
window.

He stared at the birds, noticing that they all seemed
to be watching him. There were so many of them, their
ebony bodies silhouetted against a cloudless sky, their

shiny dark eyes glittering in the growing twilight. As this murder of crows began to caw, he listened as if this time he might decode whatever they'd come to tell him. But like last time, he couldn't make sense of it. Was it another warning, one he was going to wish that he'd heeded?

Laughing to himself, he closed the window and finished his dishes. He didn't really believe the crows were a portent of what was to come this time—any more than last time. His grandmother had, though. He remembered watching her cross herself and mumble a prayer as if the crows were an omen of something sinister on its way. As it turned out, she'd been right.

At almost forty, Jasper could scoff all he wanted, even as a bad feeling settled deep in his belly. That feeling only worsened as the crows suddenly all took flight as if their work was done.

Over the next few days, he would remember the evening the crows appeared. It was the same day Leviathan Nash arrived in Buckhorn, Montana, to open his shop in the old carriage house and strange things had begun to happen—even before people started dying.

Don't miss
Before Buckhorn *by B.J. Daniels,*
available February 2022 wherever
HQN books and ebooks are sold.

HQNBooks.com

HARLEQUIN

Heartfelt or thrilling, passionate or uplifting—Harlequin is more than just happily-ever-after.

With twelve different series to choose from and new books available every month, you are sure to find stories that will move you, uplift you, inspire and delight you.

SIGN UP FOR THE HARLEQUIN NEWSLETTER

Be the first to hear about great new reads and exciting offers!

Harlequin.com/newsletters